SOMEONE TO CHERISH YOU

A H Bracken

For Michael - my favourite thing
about Yorkshire, and quite simply the love of my life.

And for Siâni - without you, there'd be
no 'December', no 'H&J' and no 'Cherish'.
I couldn't do this without you.

Prologue

He walked into the living room to be greeted by a dazzling smile. Frankie was almost nine months pregnant, and seeing her sitting on the sofa with her feet up, he once again questioned the sense of going to a wedding, particularly in the middle of a freezing and wet January. Despite broaching the subject on several occasions, she was not to be dissuaded. Emboldened by how settled she seemed to be, surrounded by cushions and the crochet blanket her grandma had made years ago, he decided to have another go.

"Are you really up to this wedding, darling? I mean, it's an awful day, and you're looking so tired. Surely an afternoon with your feet up in front of the log burner is better for you and the baby?" As he spoke, the look on Frankie's face made it clear what her response would be.

"No, I have to be there. Help me up. I need to get ready."

However, the baby had other ideas, and as Frankie gingerly got up on her feet, the warm sensation that greeted her was unexpected.

"I think my waters have broken," she said quietly, the colour draining from her face as the reality of what was about to happen sunk in.

The case was packed – Frankie was nothing if not prepared

– and the journey to the hospital wasn't going to be too long, even on a Saturday afternoon. As the car wound its way through the town towards the local hospital, Frankie watched the world go by through the rain droplets on the windows, taking in the moody pewter grey sky. It reminded her of her first few weeks in Yorkshire. She hadn't expected things to move this quickly; in fact, she hadn't expected her life to have followed this path to motherhood or the completeness she now felt.

In her little corner of utopia, she had experienced a life that she could have only dreamed about two years ago, and she frequently had. But now she had it all – the perfect man, a heavenly home, a fabulous family and friends, and in just a few hours, the baby she had so often yearned for. Life was good, even if, at this moment in time, the waves of excruciating pain were perhaps something she could do without.

The journey to the hospital was uneventful, but the weather was appalling, the rain lashing against the windscreen and the wipers struggling even at full pelt to keep the view clear. Trying to stay as still and calm as she could, remembering all her breathing exercises, Frankie closed her eyes for a few minutes and drifted back in time, her head full of the memories of her grandma.

The ping of his mobile brought her back to reality. "Oh hell! The wedding…."

"Don't worry, I let them know we're on our way - to the hospital, not the church," winked her fiancé with a wry smile.

Frankie relaxed, her disappointment at not being able to attend a wedding she'd so looked forward to tempered by the imminent arrival of the baby within her and all that entailed. She looked at her phone and the date on the screen, 16 January – the second anniversary of her grandmother's funeral.

"If it's a girl, I'd like to call her Elizabeth ..." Frankie said nervously as they drove up to the maternity entrance, where a team was waiting for her at the doorway, ready to take her in. Elizabeth, she thought.... and with the lights, the nurses and the general rush of what was going on, her thoughts floated back to that day, a day when everything began to change.

Chapter 1

Two Years Earlier...

The wind blew hard into Frankie Gleane's face as she stood in the churchyard and watched her grandmother's coffin as it was lowered into the grave. Tears streamed down her face, and she reached out instinctively for her partner Robert's hand to find it firmly tucked into his coat pocket. The service had been moving and beautiful, but the sadness was overwhelming for Frankie, who had been dreading this day since her grandmother passed. It was cold and wet, and Robert's refusal to hold her hand made a hard day much harder still.

The day had started much like any other. Robert had risen with the alarm, showered and bolted to the office without so much as a word, and Frankie had the house to herself as she showered and then dressed in the most comfortable clothing she could find. After a light breakfast of a cereal bar and coffee, she was sat at her desk in her study by 9 am, ready to begin working through the list of calls she needed to make.

Frankie worked for Urqharts, a local firm that specialised in home improvements. Her job was to make unsolicited calls to unsuspecting households and ask them if they needed double glazing or any other manner of external work done. It was a tough job that required a thick skin - something which Frankie simply didn't possess - and most days involved the joys of people either shouting at her or hanging up. It was demoralising and lonely, but it was a job she could do from home, and with all of the disruption caused by the pandemic, it had provided steady employment throughout. After so many months of lockdown and relative isolation, the concept of getting in the car and driving any distance to an office was unappealing. It wasn't much of a job. It was primarily commission-based, meaning Frankie needed to put in the hours to make a decent amount of money, and that was sometimes hard to do, hence the reason she was working on the day of her grandmother's funeral. In contrast, Robert, Frankie's partner for almost seven years, was a car salesman and made very good money. He never missed an opportunity to remind Frankie how much he earned, and it was a constant source of tension between the couple.

All things considered, Frankie had a good morning, and at 11 am, she logged off and started to get ready. Robert was picking her up at 12 to take her to the church. She took a cup of coffee with her upstairs to the bedroom and sank onto the bed, assailed with a wave of grief. She still couldn't believe her grandma was gone. It had happened so quickly - one minute, she was off out to the supermarket, and the next, she was in the hospital with a chest infection. And then, three days after she was admitted and in the early hours of the morning, she had died, alone and afraid, something Frankie felt an unsettling affinity with. The doctors hadn't expected it, and it was a complete shock for everyone.

The soft, smart shift dress went on quickly, and a stylish pair of black high heeled shoes completed the look. Frankie's shoulder-length blond hair was tied back in a simple ponytail, and in the light of the bedroom, her pale skin looked almost translucent, dotted with freckles and with no make-up to cover them. Frankie stood in front of the mirror and appraised herself, quickly concluding she looked pretty good, all things considered. It made her feel uncomfortable that she tried as hard as she did to look nice for Robert, but he rarely noticed her anymore, and it hurt.

An engine roar outside signalled Robert's arrival, and it wasn't long before Frankie heard the front door click open.

"You ready, Frank?" he shouted up the stairs.

"Yeah. I'm coming down now," Frankie replied, grabbing her handbag and making for the stairs, keen to avoid irritating Robert, who was always punctual and expected everyone around him to be the same. She thought she heard him speak again but couldn't catch what he said.

"You look … nice," he said, briefly looking up from his phone.

"Thanks." Frankie knew he hadn't looked at her properly, and the familiar feeling of disappointment settled in.

Robert stood and watched as Frankie struggled to get her coat on, not offering any assistance and simply looking at his watch as if to hurry her up. Within a few minutes, they were in the car and on their way to the church.

The sight of the coffin in the back of the hearse made Frankie cry, and she didn't stop at any point through the funeral service. Losing her grandma had been more painful than she could ever have imagined. They had been extremely close, and if Frankie ever needed anyone to talk to, her grandma had always been there for her.

The funeral had been planned down to the tiniest detail by Elizabeth Gleane herself, ever keen to control every facet of her life, and seemingly death, wherever possible. The hymns, the flowers, the readings and even the outfit she was wearing to be laid to rest – every detail noted in her will years ago.

She had impeccable taste, and the funeral was a beautiful and moving tribute to a woman who had left a gaping hole in the lives of those who loved her.

As the funeral service finished and the congregation moved out into the churchyard, Robert's phone rang, and he stalked away from the crowd to take the call.

"You'd think he could have turned that off for a couple of hours," said Martin Gleane, Frankie's dad. "How he can be so important that he can't step away for a funeral is beyond me?"

"He's probably negotiating a sale, Martin. It's a cutthroat industry he's in, you know," said Jane, Frankie's generous-spirited mother, effectively closing Martin down to avoid any scrutiny of Frankie's relationship on such a difficult day. "You look well, dear … and very glamorous in that frock."

"Thanks, Mum. I love this dress. I never thought I'd be wearing it to Grandma's funeral, though." She watched Robert on the other side of the churchyard, talking into his phone and looking around to make sure he was alone. There was no way he was negotiating a sale, thought Frankie sadly, turning her attention back to her parents and catching them up.

Robert marched back over to the group. "I'll need to shoot off in a bit. I need to get back to the showroom. Can Frankie get a lift with you to the wake?"

The way he spoke about Frankie like she wasn't there was something Frankie herself no longer noticed, but it was a constant source of irritation for Jane and Martin. In fact, there was quite a lot about Robert that they were less than keen on. But Frankie seemed to love him, leaving them with no choice but to tolerate the relationship for as long as it lasted.

"Why don't we ask Frankie?" said Martin, looking at Robert with unmasked disrespect. "Frankie, are you happy to come to the wake with us while your boyfriend goes back to work?"

Frankie felt uncomfortable and hated the friction between Robert and her parents. This was just another awkward interaction she had to navigate. "Yes, that's fine. Will you come to the internment, though, Robert? I'll need you there for that...."

"Okay," Robert replied, with so little enthusiasm, it was evident that as far as he was concerned, the whole occasion was a massive chore best avoided. "But I need to be away from here by two at the latest," he added, checking his watch to reinforce the point.

Jane shot Martin a look, and Frankie tried hard to stare at the ground as they all moved with the crowd towards the grave for the internment.

The wind was blowing hard across the churchyard, and Frankie was upset that Robert wasn't staying for the wake. She needed his support on this of all days, and the sadness ramped up to annoyance for a fraction of a second. But the feeling was quickly replaced by the usual apathy, a complete lack of control over what he did or who he did it with

As the vicar concluded the graveside service and people began to shift and move towards the car park, Robert shot off with barely a goodbye, jumped into his car and sped away, his engine roaring noisily. Frankie left alone at the graveside, threw a single flower onto the coffin and said goodbye to her grandma for the last time.

Jane came and stood alongside her. "Come on, love. Let's get you to the pub."

Frankie nodded and wiped her eyes. Then, together, Martin, Jane and their daughter walked to the car and drove the short distance to the wake.

In the pub, it was noisy, but it was warm, and Frankie

found a nice spot in a busy corner so she could chat to people as they passed and didn't need to move much in her heels. They looked amazing, but standing around in them unthinkable. They were tools of toe torture. She sat and watched as people talked, and there was a lot of hugging. People were crying and laughing; there were so many people that loved Elizabeth Gleane - the pub was packed, and there was an equal balance of sadness and joy as people remembered all of the things that made Frankie's grandma as wonderful as she was.

Frankie didn't need to move, except for grabbing a plate of food from the buffet. People stopped by and chatted; Martin bought her drinks, and, strangely, she found herself having a lovely time and enjoying reminiscing about her grandma. But her heart sank when she saw her Aunty Jean near the bar, and she braced herself as Jean made eye contact, approached and sat down for a chat.

Jean was Jane's older and far less diplomatic sister. Single since she was in her late 40s and now happily living with her nine cats, Jean was cynical and opinionated to a fault. She also had the knack of cutting straight to the point with the maximum offence and was most definitely not one to mince her words.

"Frankie, dear, you look exhausted. How are you getting on? Where's that errant boyfriend of yours?"

"He had to go back to work, and I'm fine, thanks. How are you?" Frankie knew she was in for a heavy dose of Jean's opinion about her life, and she braced for impact.

"Oh, I'm okay dear, same as ever, you know me! But I do worry about you. Your poor mum is beside herself fretting about when you'll get married. You're no age to be this - well - childless, dear. Your poor mum is desperate for some grandchildren. You're not exactly a spring chicken now, are you dear?" Jean placed her hand on Frankie's knee to soften the blow of her words; It didn't work.

"No, I suppose I'm not," Frankie replied, fully aware that she was edging further into her 30s than she ever imagined without being a mother. "But having children isn't something that Robert and I are bothered about. I'm sure Mum understands."

"I'm sure that's what you tell yourself, dear, but no one can ignore their biological clock forever. It's a lesson I had to learn the hard way. I know your mum is nervous to talk to you about it. I've told her she needs to just cut to the chase, but she won't. She says she doesn't want to upset you. Ridiculous if you ask me. Have you thought about adoption? There are some lovely babies in the Far East. You could probably get a couple of those if you wanted? Although I'm not sure you're cut out for motherhood, dear. Far too much hard work for someone that can't keep her man at her side."

Frankie wanted the floor to open up and Jean to drop through it. Instead, the insensitivity of Jean's words cut through her like a knife through butter. She was desperate for children and had been for years now. But Robert didn't want any, and of course, it was true that he was always somewhere else, with someone else. She knew that better than anyone, and she didn't need her Aunty Jean to point it out.

Fighting back her tears, she replied, "We haven't talked about having children yet, Jean. Robert is very busy with his job." It was a lie. A big lie. They had discussed having children when they first met, and Robert had been very clear he didn't want any. But she had foolishly believed she could change his mind. Seven years on, and he was steadfast in his refusal to even so much as talk about it. She looked for support and spotted her mum, who immediately realised that her daughter needed rescuing and bounded over to help.

"Ah Jean, there you are. Come and help me sort out the buffet, would you? Martin's no use, bless him.   Far too upset." She shot Jean a look that left little room for disagreement, and thankfully, Jean stood and allowed herself to be steered towards the buffet and away from Frankie. Jane looked over her shoulder and winked, and Frankie mouthed "Thank you" across the room.

The house was in darkness when Frankie arrived home around 5 pm. She had wanted to leave earlier but, having been abandoned by Robert and entirely dependent on her parents for transport, she had to wait until they were ready to go. Martin wanted to say goodbye to everyone personally and seemed unwilling to end his dear mother's wake. So, it had dragged on, and by the time Jane had managed to extract him from the pub, even the landlord looked grateful to put an end to the melancholy and open his pub up to happy people as soon as possible.

As she turned to get out of the car, Martin spoke. "Before you go, love, I've got something to give you." He reached into his pocket and held out a pink envelope with flowers on the back - her grandma's favourite stationery.

"It's from your grandma. She asked me to give this to you if anything happened to her." Martin's voice broke with emotion, and he thrust the letter towards Frankie as if it were burning his skin.

"What is it?" Frankie asked, equally choked at the thought of a message from her grandma.

"You need to open it and have a read, sweetheart," said Jane from the driver's seat. "It's something your grandma wanted to do for you. But maybe open it tomorrow, darling, when Robert's gone to work. It's been a long and emotional day, and you need some rest now."

"Okay, I will," agreed Frankie, stowing the precious envelope into her bag.

The effort of walking from the car to the front door was immense after an entire afternoon in the shoes, and by the time she opened the door and turned to wave at her parents, she was kicking the shoes into the hallway. The letter was, for the moment at least, forgotten. She hung up her coat and switched on a few lights around the house. There was no sign of Robert, but she wasn't expecting him home for a couple of hours yet. He was rarely home before seven any night, and if he'd had a busy afternoon, he could be later even than that. She knew she needed to change out of the dress but couldn't face climbing the stairs, so instead, she went to the kitchen, pulled out a bowl of leftover lasagne from the fridge and microwaved it. Next, she poured a glass of red wine, laid everything on a tray and carried it carefully into the lounge.

Picking at the lasagne with her fork, she flicked through the TV channels, trying to find something interesting to watch. Finally, selecting a property renovation show, she settled herself in for a couple of hours in front of the TV and enjoyed her meal and the glass of wine.

She had always had an interest in property renovation, and when she was younger, she had hoped to build up a sum of money to invest in a property to renovate and grow from there. She worked at the gallery in town, earning a good salary as the manager and she was on target to start looking for a property when Robert came along. But then everything changed because he didn't share her passion; instead, she invested her savings and the equity from the flat she owned into Robert's house, moving in quickly after they met.

By 10 pm, eyes heavy and desperate for sleep, Frankie checked her phone and found nothing from Robert. So, she tidied up her dinner things and turned everything off except the hallway light, so Robert could see when he came into the house later.

She grabbed a glass of water and climbed the stairs, pulled

the dress over her head and threw it on the chair.

A few minutes later, she had washed her face and brushed her teeth. She walked back across the landing to the bedroom and climbed into bed at last, her body instantly soothed by the softness of the mattress and the warmth of the duvet.

Within minutes, she fell into a deep sleep and didn't hear Robert's noisy arrival at midnight. He roared the car onto the drive, banged the front door closed and shouted to see if Frankie was awake, but Frankie didn't stir. Standing in the bedroom doorway and seeing his partner sleeping peacefully, he checked his phone and, smiling broadly, picked up a photo message from the woman he'd spent the afternoon with.

Chapter 2

The alarm went off at 7.30 am, and Frankie turned over and found herself alone, something that was becoming more usual. The house was quiet, and she knew Robert must have left for work already. It made her sad that they spent so little time together, but he loved his job, and Frankie was happy about that.

She lay for a while and enjoyed the quiet and the warmth of her bed. It was January, and although the heating was on, the house still felt colder outside the duvet than under it. There was the distant sound of a siren outside the window, and occasionally a neighbour's car would pass the house. They lived in a small cul-de-sac, and there wasn't usually a great deal of traffic. The biggest problems stemmed from the little children playing out on their bikes on the long summer evenings. Robert had turned into the street and nearly ran over a little one more than once. It wasn't an issue in the winter, but even so, it scared Frankie. She often asked Robert to drive a little more slowly but to no avail.

With no Robert around to distract her, Frankie's mind drifted to the previous day, and she began to wonder where he had needed to go with such importance, he would miss her grandma's funeral. A small alarm bell started to sound in the back of her mind, but she steadfastly ignored it, determined to see the best in Robert, despite his long list of past infidelities. He had promised he was done with it all and that he would be faithful to her, and if they were to have any future together, she had to try and believe him.

Noticing the time, Frankie leapt from the bed and headed for the shower. There were calls to make, and every minute mattered if she was going to hit her revenue target this month.

Carrying her cup of coffee into the study, Frankie noticed the post had been delivered, and she placed the coffee on the side table in the hall and opened up the porch. There were several envelopes, primarily for Robert. But one was addressed to both of them, and it looked like their joint account bank statement, so she picked up her coffee, went through to the study and settled herself into her big leather chair. She sliced open the envelope using the sword-shaped opener she had inherited from her grandfather and pulled the statement out. It was pretty unremarkable, a long list of grocery purchases, the mortgage, a couple of insurance direct debits. And then she saw it. A transaction for £279.78 and the description simply said 'The Belmont'.

At first, Frankie assumed it was just something she had forgotten, her memory getting worse by the day, according to Robert at least. But, as the morning moved into afternoon, the transaction from 'The Belmont' played on her mind more and more, and so eventually, she gave in to her curiosity and had another look. Despite wracking her brain, she couldn't think of anything it could be and decided it must be something Robert had charged to the joint account by mistake. Intending to leave it there, she placed the statement to the side of her desk and got back to the tedious job at hand, dialling the next number on her list.

Ten phone calls and nine rejections and insults later, it was time for a break. There was only so much abuse a person could take before a cup of tea and a biscuit was needed. As she went to stand up, she caught sight of the statement again and paused. Something wasn't right, and she couldn't shake the sensation that she needed to know more. Discarding her plans for refreshment, instead, she logged into the online banking and scrolled down to the transaction. She clicked on it, and it opened up some more detail.

'The Belmont Hotel, Accommodation & Sundries'

Frankie noticed the date was three weeks ago. She worked back through the last couple of weeks and smiled when she realised, with relief, that three weeks ago, Robert had been on an overnight convention in Bristol. So that must be it, she thought, smiling, and she got up and made herself that cup of tea.

Returning to her desk a few minutes later, munching on a digestive biscuit, she was in a different frame of mind. She opened up the internet again and searched for the hotel. Sure enough, there was a hotel of that name in Bristol. And that should have been a relief. But it wasn't, and the nagging uncertainty was still there, pressing her to dig further.

Before she could talk herself out of it, Frankie picked up the phone and called the hotel.

"Oh, hi. I wonder if you can help me? I'm just running through our accounts, and I need to double-check that a member of our team stayed at your hotel on 4th January."

"Of course, if you can give me the name, please, and I'll check the system and see for you," replied the receptionist.

"Thank you. His name is Robert Hughes. He stayed for one night, I believe?" Frankie's heart was pounding in her chest as she waited for the receptionist to check the system.

"Ah yes, here it is. One night, dinner, bed and breakfast…." As the receptionist spoke, Frankie's heart calmed a little. But the receptionist wasn't finished. "Booked under the name of

Mr and Mrs Hughes. Is that all you need?"

Frankie was stunned and couldn't reply.

"Hello? Are you there? Is that all you need?" asked the receptionist, confused by the unexpected silence.

"Hello, sorry! Yes, I'm still here…" Frankie tried to sound calm despite the storm raging inside her. "Can I just check? Did Mrs Hughes stay too? Or was the booking made for two, but only one arrived?" She knew she was grasping at straws now, but she needed this not to be true. Not again.

"Give me a moment … Yes. Mrs Hughes did stay too. She had a massage and a facial in the spa. Of course, she paid for that separately."

Frankie managed a polite thank you and put the phone down. The room seemed to be spinning, and she held her head in her hands to try and steady herself. How could this be happening? How could Robert be unfaithful to her again? Anger bubbled up, and this time it wasn't extinguished by the excuses she always made for his behaviour. Excuses were simply not enough to overwrite the hurt she was feeling.

Frankie couldn't work, and once the shock had subsided sufficiently to be able to breathe, she had called in and told her manager, Simon, that she would be off sick for the rest of the day. He hadn't sounded impressed, but Frankie could not have cared less, her world crumbling all around her.

She spent the afternoon moving between the kitchen, lounge and the bedroom, unable to settle in any space, a constant potential dialogue with Robert running through her mind, over and over again. She didn't know whether to confront him or just accept that this was her life now. As she wrestled between fight and defeat, she became more and more exhausted and eventually, she fell asleep.

The familiar roar of Robert's car woke her, and she found herself lying in total darkness, having presumably been asleep for hours. And then the reality of her day washed over her, and the fact that Robert was opening the front door sent a chill up her back. This was it. She had to decide whether to take Robert's behaviour lying down and set aside every shred of dignity she possessed or whether she would fight for her relationship, and more importantly, for her sense of self.

"Frank? Are you home?" Robert called up the stairs.

"Yes. I'm just coming down," Frankie replied, still debating the next move and hoping she would decide before reaching the bottom step.

As she walked into the kitchen and saw him standing there, pouring a glass of whiskey, she knew what she had to do. There was still enough spirit left in her to stand up for herself, and she stood a little taller as she spoke.

"Who did you go to Bristol with?" she asked, holding his eye contact and looking strong and in control, despite her whole body shaking like a leaf.

"What? Why do you care? It was weeks ago!" he laughed, dismissing her.

"I care because I think you were there with a woman." Frankie spoke slowly and clearly, careful to measure every word, fearful of Robert's ability to manipulate what she said.

He looked a little ruffled suddenly but took a sip of whiskey and held her gaze.

"There were loads of women at the hotel, Frank. It was a convention." His tone was condescending.

He was trying to distract her, demean her argument. She wasn't going to stand for it. Not this time. "I have spoken to the hotel, and they told me that Mrs Hughes stayed there too. And apparently, she had a massage and a facial." Frankie crossed her arms, hoping to look strong and defiant and shield herself from what she knew was coming next.

"Have you been checking up on me? I told you, you could trust me; that should have been good enough for you. How dare you go checking up on me."

His insistence didn't land as effectively as Robert had hoped, and Frankie - clear on the facts this time and therefore less inclined to relent - stood her ground. "You charged the room to the joint account, Robert. What do you expect if you are daft enough to do that?"

Robert's eyes were shining with rage, and he slammed his glass down on the counter, splashing whiskey over his hand and the cuff of his suit jacket. Frankie knew this would be where it would start to get tricky, but there was nowhere to go, and she didn't feel like running anyway.

"Okay. So, I was there with a woman. What are you going to do about it, Frankie? I mean, think about it. It's not like you have ever left me, is it? You get cross, say you're all hurt, and I say I'm sorry. Rinse and repeat, Frank. Rinse and repeat!"

Frankie stood perfectly still, her face expressionless. She knew he was right, and it burned inside her. She had always turned the other cheek, time and time again. And now he was expecting her to do it again.

"And let's be honest, Frank, it's not like you're going to leave me, is it? I mean, it's not like you have anywhere to go. If you did, you'd have left years ago." Robert stared at her, waiting for his words to pierce her frozen exterior and yield a reaction.

But Frankie didn't speak. Frustrated at her lack of response, Robert poured another whiskey and resumed his hard stare.

"So, what now? Are you going to cook me some dinner, or shall we get a takeaway?" he asked, entirely blind to the turmoil raging with Frankie's mind.

"Eat what you want. I'm not hungry," said Frankie quietly, and she turned and walked away, leaving Robert alone with his whiskey, a self-satisfied smile dancing across his lips.

Their paths didn't cross again that night. Frankie moved her things into the guest room, and the only contact she had with Robert was him shouting goodnight as he went to bed. Once he had passed out, Frankie crept downstairs and poured herself a small whiskey, grabbed a bag of peanuts and her handbag and crept back upstairs again.

In the safety of the guest room, she weighed up her options. The process didn't take long because Frankie didn't have many options to consider; it was either stay with him or go and live with her parents. She was financially tied to Robert and had no spare cash to rent a place of her own. It didn't come as much of a surprise to her this evening; she and Robert had had similar conversations many times before during the course of his many infidelities.

"I wish Grandma were still here," she said aloud, feeling the enormous hole in her life that her grandmother's passing had created. "She would know what to do," she said to the big brown teddy bear on the chair by the window. And then Frankie remembered the letter, somehow forgotten in the drama of the night before and the day she'd had. She rifled through her bag and retrieved the pink, flowery envelope and was all set to open it when she stopped herself. What if this made her feel worse? What if this just opened up even more grief and sadness. Could she take that tonight, after everything that had happened?

Deciding that she needed to hear from her grandma even if it made her feel worse, she carefully undid the envelope, trying to preserve it as much as possible. Inside was a letter, and she unfolded it slowly and began to read.

My dearest Frankie

As much of a cliche as this is - if you're reading this, then I'm gone. I'm in a better place, and you can be sure I've found your grandad, and I'm happy as can be again. But there was always one thing that bothered me about dying, and Frankie, my darling, it was leaving you.

Tears rolled down Frankie's face, making it hard to read, but she wiped them away and carried on.

I'm going to be honest with you because there's nothing to stop me now! This needs to be said, so I'm saying it. Robert is not good for you. He doesn't make you happy, and you know it as well as I do. All those hours we spent talking and me holding you were all about him, and the fact he doesn't cherish you. And you should be cherished, my darling girl.

Now I know you love him. Goodness knows you must do to stick with him. And maybe you see something in him that the rest of us don't. But I'm worried for you, and I want to give you a way to find out exactly what that man is made of and give you a chance to thrive.

So, I've left the keys to my old cottage up in Yorkshire with your dad, and I've also set aside some money for you to have. But the deal is you go when the time is right, and you'll know when that is, my darling - no one can decide that for you. So, when the time is right, I want you to get in your car, drive yourself up to that cottage and stay there for as long as it takes. Give that man a chance to miss you and realise what he's got. As I'm gone, I'll be honest and say I'd rather you didn't take him back, but that's your decision, my dear.

And while you're there, I want you to sort out my cottage, do a bit of improvement, like those programmes you watch on the telly. Then, if Robert comes up there and sweeps you off your feet, you can sell it and use it to start your property empire. But until he does, you work on getting yourself happy again. Because my darling girl, you are still in there. Your heart isn't happy, and I want you to see whether you can change that.

Your Dad has all the keys and the money and everything you need. He doesn't know why mind. It's up to you if you want to tell him.

And that's it. That's what I wanted to say. Oh, except that you have always been the brightest star in my life, my angel, my ray of sunshine. Don't cry too much for me, sweet girl, because I'm back with your grandad now, and I'm happy. Now it's time for you to be happy. Find the light that used to be in your eyes. Make sure you find someone to cherish you. You are so precious, my little Frankie, and you deserve to shine like the star you are.

I love you
Grandma xxx

Frankie broke into deep sobs, and her grief came pouring out all at once, overwhelming her. She lay down, clutching the letter to her chest and allowing sadness to envelop her. She needed to feel it, and as she cried into her pillow, her eyes became heavy, and she soon drifted into a deep and healing sleep.

Chapter 3

The winter sun streamed through a gap in the curtains, and Frankie stirred. The rustle of paper made her open her eyes, and she realised that she had fallen asleep clutching the letter to her chest. For a second or two, she felt warm and secure, and then the reality of her situation fell on her like an unbearable weight. Her whole body hurt, primarily due to the firm mattress on the guest bed, but also because of the argument with Robert, and of course, the letter, reminding her of what she had lost, but giving her license to imagine a different future. So much to think about, so many decisions to make, so little time to decide her next steps.

The house was silent, but that didn't mean anything. Robert could well be home, either still asleep or downstairs reading his paper. It was Saturday, and he sometimes went into work, but he rarely told Frankie when he would be working weekends. He pretty much came and went as he pleased, and Frankie fell into step with whatever rhythm he set for himself. It had always been like that, and it had never occurred to Frankie how selfish it was - until now. Lying there, unsure whether Robert was in the house, and still hurt and angry after his blatant admission of the affair, and the fact she had no idea where he was and whether she could even get to the bathroom without having to face him, made her anger grow just a little more, feeling like a prisoner in her own bed.

She lay there for a few minutes, listening intently for any sound that might indicate Robert was home. The longer she lay there, the heavier her body felt, as if it knew she was scared to move. But nature was calling, and Frankie needed to get to the bathroom, so she was left with no option other than to get up.

The trip to the bathroom was uneventful; there was no sign of Robert in the house. A quick check out the window told her he had not long gone into work; the driveway where he parked his car was the one remaining dry spot on an otherwise drizzly, wet morning. Knowing he was gone, Frankie pulled on her big fleecy dressing gown and went downstairs to make herself some coffee. The letter was tucked in her pocket and felt like it was burning through to her thigh; such was her awareness of it and the decision she now faced.

When Robert had brought her to his home the first time, Frankie had loved the open plan kitchen family room as soon as she saw it. And when he had suggested she move in with him, she had been most excited about this room, and the idea of a lazy weekend breakfast settled on the big squashy sofa and looking out over the garden. But it was impossible to ignore how much this particular breakfast did not fit that romantic image. Alone and lost in a whirlwind of thoughts about her life, Frankie felt sad, and the weather outside was very much on message with the drizzle from earlier now upgraded to full and persistent rain. She settled herself into the sofa cushions, pulling a blanket over her legs and watching a tiny robin as it walked in front of the patio doors, peered inside, pecked at the ground and then flew off quickly.

The coffee was too hot to drink, but the cup provided extra

warmth, and Frankie blew on the hot liquid as she clasped the cup with both hands. The words 'Happy Together' were emblazoned across it, and Frankie could see it peeking through the gaps in her fingers. However, the words felt empty and meaningless, and she lay her head back against the sofa's plush, deep red fabric, eyes closed and breathing deeply.

She knew it was time to weigh up her options, particularly now, thanks to her grandma, she actually had some options. For the first time in her relationship, there was an escape route if she needed it, and although this would have felt like a relief to many people, it felt like defeat to Frankie. So many years had been given over to Robert and creating a life with him. To walk away now would mean those years were wasted.

But all of that said, a tiny part of Frankie knew she had to make a stand or life would never be anything she could stomach. She sipped her coffee and wiped away a single tear. She didn't want to cry; she wanted to make everything disappear. All of Robert's other women just needed to go away, and then everything could be perfect again.

Deep inside, she knew it would never happen. Robert was unable to be faithful, and he would never change. Frankie reached into her pocket and pulled out the letter, smoothing the creases and rereading it. The cottage was miles away and perched high on a cliff, looking out over Robin Hoods Bay. It was old and run down, or at least it had been the last time Frankie had been there, and that was ten years ago when her grandma had moved down to live with her parents after Grandad had died. It must be in a worse state now, Frankie thought, taking a swig of coffee and placing the cup down on the glass table. Her dad had been up a few times to keep the cottage and grounds maintained, and there was an arrangement with a local farmer to keep the grass cut and the gardens neat. But beyond that, it had sat empty for a decade, cold and unloved. It needed someone to breathe new life into it for sure. But could that be Frankie? Could she do it? Did she have the courage to go up there and do the work the cottage needed?

So many questions and all Frankie could feel in response was doubt. She closed her eyes, trying to picture her grandma as if to comfort her in this moment of extreme emotional difficulty. And with little effort, there she was, sat in her favourite chair in the sunroom, knitting without a care and smiling lovingly at Frankie. But then, a wave of grief joined the emotional maelstrom and Frankie could do nothing but allow the tears to fall and settle gently on the cushion behind her head, eyes still closed, not wanting to lose sight of her precious grandma again.

"If nothing ever changes, dear, why would anything ever change?" thought Frankie, as if channelling her grandma for a moment. It was a phrase that Elizabeth Gleane had used repeatedly to Frankie since it became clear that Robert had an eye for the ladies. Elizabeth had been certain that Frankie needed to do something to change her life; she had more than hinted as much on many occasions. And now, letter in hand and relationship in tatters, those words came to Frankie's mind like a well-timed flashlight on a dark night.

"I need to change," she said aloud. "I need to do something to get my life back on track again." The concept made absolute sense to Frankie, and she eased herself up and stood in front of the patio doors. The rain was coming down harder now, and the clouds were dark and heavy in the sky. She looked at her reflection in the glass. Her hair was dishevelled, her face pale with puffy eyes and tear-stained cheeks. The dressing gown made her look enormous, but there was no disputing that Frankie was carrying more weight than she was comfortable with even below the dressing gown. Once upon a time, all Frankie had ever wanted was for Robert to look at her and desire her. But times had changed, and Frankie was forced to acknowledge that in reality, after all he'd done, she didn't really care whether Robert liked what he saw anymore.

"Where have I gone?" she asked her reflection. "How do I get back to my old self?" The reflection simply stared back at her and didn't answer. Instead, the rain on the glass made it look like Frankie was crying heavy, grey tears, and for a moment, she felt herself falling back into the defeated state she had been in just moments ago. But something pulled her back. "Something needs to change," she said again. And at that moment, facing herself in the glass and with nothing left to lose, Frankie knew what she had to do. It would only be for a few months, and it might just be the kick start the relationship needed.

Pulling her phone from the dressing gown pocket, Frankie dialled her parent's number and waited for them to answer.

"Hi, Dad."

"Hello, darling! How are you feeling today?" replied Martin, his voice reflecting his ever-present concern for his daughter.

"Oh, I'm…." Frankie was about to give her usual platitudes, reassuring her dad that she was okay despite being upset, but today, something was different. She wanted to be honest. "Actually, Dad, I'm not feeling very good. Robert and I are having some problems again."

"Oh, I'm sorry, love. Is there anything we can do for you? Do you need anything brought around? Any shopping?"

"No, it's fine, Dad. It's just, well, I opened Grandma's letter…." She trailed off, unsure whether to tell her father about Robert's latest affair being the catalyst for her accepting the offer.

"Ah, I see. Well, it's only to be used when you need it,

Frankie darling. So, you don't need to race off to Yorkshire immediately."

"Well, the thing is…Robert and I need a bit of a break from each other, I think. I don't want to go into it, but we've had a row, and I think it might be a good idea for me to go away for a bit." There. It was said. Frankie felt brave and in control. On the other hand, Martin seemed to be panicking, and Frankie could hear him summoning Jane to the phone, his hand clearly over the phone to silence his voice as he called in reinforcements.

Frankie continued, "But I think I need to go today. Would that be okay, do you think?"

"Hello dear, it's your mother," said Jane, making Frankie smile. As if it could be anyone else!

"Hi, Mum. I take it Dad has just told you I'm thinking of going away for a bit?"

"Yes, he has. And I want to know what that man has done to make you think this is a good idea? I was never in favour of Elizabeth and your dad putting this little plan together, like some kind of twisted rescue mission. You shouldn't need to go gallivanting across the UK on some kind of crusade to save your relationship, Francesca."

Frankie wasn't surprised by what her mum was saying, and on some level, she agreed. It was crazy to be leaving Robert when in reality, it was him who should be running away with his tail between his legs.

"Maybe you're right," she replied, her resolve wavering for a moment.

"Now hang on a minute," said Martin, giving away the fact that the phone was on loudspeaker. "I don't know what Robert has done, but I can make a pretty good guess based on his previous form. That man needs to understand what he has got there, and your grandmother knew very well the only way to make him see you was to help you disappear for a bit."

"I don't think…" began Jane, but Martin was having none of it.

"Jane, you are too protective of Frankie. I know you love her but just look at how little respect that man shows our girl. She needs to get away, get some sea air in her lungs and realise she is worth much more than how he treats her."

Frankie winced and leapt to Robert's defence. "Dad, Robert isn't a bad man. He is good to me in many ways…."

"I'm just telling you what your grandma thought. And to be honest, it makes good sense to me. You were a bright and vibrant woman who had bags of confidence until you met that man. You would never have stood for the kind of nonsense that Robert throws at you. You've changed, Frankie. Your expectations have dropped. Coincidence? I don't think so."

Everyone fell silent for a moment as they reflected on Martin's words. Frankie knew there was at least a fragment of truth in what he was saying, although the raw honesty was hard to accept.

"Do you want to go?" Jane asked, breaking the silence. "I mean, are things there so bad that you feel this will help?"

Frankie thought for a moment. It was pretty bad. Another affair, total indifference to how it made Frankie feel, and worst of all, Robert had finally been honest enough to tell her he believed he could get away with it over and over again. There was nothing left. If she stayed here and turned the other cheek, she would sink lower into an abyss of sadness, resentment and self-loathing, and Robert would drift further and further away. She couldn't bear it.

"I have to do something, Mum. I don't want to carry on like this," Frankie replied simply, rechecking her reflection in the window and wincing at how squidgy and wrecked she looked.

"And you believe it's a relationship worth saving?" asked Martin, Jane tutting her disapproval in the background.

"I'm not sure, Dad. But unless I put some distance between Robert and me, I'll never be able to think it through clearly."

"Well, it sounds like you've made your mind up. Your Mum and I can drop the keys around in an hour and help you pack up the car. Are you sure this is what you want?" said Martin, eager to give his daughter one final chance to change her mind before the wheels were set in motion.

Frankie said nothing for a moment, weighing up her feelings and looking around the room and at her life. Could she do this? Should she do this? She looked at Robert's cabinet full of sporting trophies from his youth and Robert's wine rack. She took in the abstract painting over the sofa, which she hated, but he wanted, so he bought it anyway. And then she saw the whiskey glass on the counter next to the sink. The glass he had held in his hand as he told her how convinced he was that she would always forgive him.

"I'm sure," said Frankie, barely audible.

There was no response for a moment, her parents surely staring at each other in shock and amazement. And then Martin spoke. "We'll be there in an hour. Pack what clothes and bits you'll need, and we'll get online and order some groceries to be delivered to arrive tomorrow once you've settled in."

"And do not answer your phone to anyone except us, you hear?" said Jane, worried that any contact with Robert would put an end to the possibility that Frankie might escape her rogue of a boyfriend.

"Okay." It was all Frankie could manage, but it was enough. Her parents hung up, and Frankie once again stared at her reflection. It was done. She was leaving. She turned and walked upstairs. It was time to pack, and she needed to get it done fast and before she had a chance to change her mind.

At 11.45 on the dot, precisely one hour after he hung up the phone, Martin Gleane rang the doorbell and stood waiting for his daughter to answer the door. It had been a long 60 minutes as he contemplated his daughter changing her mind and staying with a man who was disrespectful to her. Yet, even as he stood in front of the door, waiting for his daughter to open it, he remained ever so slightly unsure she would go through with it.

Inside, Frankie heard the bell ring and looked down at the suitcases at her feet. The last hour had been a battle between what she felt she should do and what felt comfortable and safe. Whilst her mind raged war on itself, thoughts screaming at each other about what she should do and the consequences of leaving and staying, Frankie had simply packed up her things. It was January, and Yorkshire was far colder than the south east, so she needed plenty of jumpers, some heavy boots for walking and a couple of books to keep her amused until she settled in. She had focused on packing the practical things she would need. Well mostly. There was a couple of dresses with matching heels thrown in, just in case.

The note she had written Robert, placed up against the dirty whiskey glass on the counter, had been written to convey precisely how Frankie felt, and it felt well written and balanced to her.

She opened the door, and Martin walked in, checking his watch to make sure there was still enough time to load the car and get her on her way before Robert arrived home. He usually finished at 12 when he worked on a Saturday, so every minute counted now if she was going to get away from his charm and persuasion.

"Are you all set?" he asked, picking up the two suitcases.

"I think so," replied Frankie, sounding anything but sure.

"Well, if you've got your keys, let's make a move. I think you should try and get away before Robert gets home. We don't want to cause a scene, do we?" In truth, Martin knew that if Robert came home and saw that Frankie was leaving, he would probably manipulate her into staying in less than five minutes.

Frankie seemed to be on message because she looked down the road to check Robert's car wasn't approaching and pulled the door closed. Martin marched ahead to open the garage and pull the car forward to put the cases inside.

Jane stepped out of Martin's car and hugged Frankie tightly. "Are you okay, love?" she asked.

"As well as can be expected," Frankie replied with a wry smile.

The garage door squeaked as it opened, and Martin got into the car while Frankie said goodbye to her mum. Within less than a minute, Martin pulled forward, loaded the suitcases, and strolled over to Frankie for his goodbye hug.

As Frankie drove out of the street, a large black BMW roared around the corner and passed her without so much as a glance from the driver, and Frankie's heart stopped for a moment. But she kept on going, and to her relief, and to the relief of her parents in the car following behind, it seemed Robert was unaware that his partner was heading in the opposite direction, travelling to a destination hundreds of miles away. Away from him and all of the hurt and disappointment he had inflicted over the last seven years.

Chapter 4

The BMW pulled onto the drive, and Robert climbed out, slamming the door shut as if to announce his arrival, albeit, and as he was about to discover, to no one. He stalked up the drive and opened the front door, but the house was silent, and the crease on his forehead indicated how unusual the lack of immediate acknowledgement from Frankie was. She always shouted hello from wherever she was in the house. But there was no sound at all.

Concerned, he moved around the ground floor, room by room, calling out Frankie's name. There was no sign of her downstairs, so he raced upstairs but she wasn't there either. The rain had stopped, so he decided to check the garden. Frankie wasn't much of a gardener, and it wasn't the time of year for it, but he was running out of options. As he moved through the kitchen, he caught sight of the envelope propped against last night's whiskey glass. As arrogant as only Robert could be, he picked up the envelope, expecting a note to say Frankie had run off to her mum and dad to lick her wounds after last night's ridiculous conversation. He pulled the letter out and began to read it.

Robert
I have left you this letter because I have gone away for a while. I

realised last night that you will never change. You will never be faithful to me, and most worryingly of all, you don't seem to see any problem with that. But I can't live that way, at least, not anymore. I have too much respect for myself to accept you treating me this way.

I will be in touch when I'm settled in. I don't know how long I'll be gone, but I hope while I'm away, we can both think about what we want out of a relationship and, therefore, whether there is anything we can salvage from what remains of ours.

Frankie

Surprised and a little upset, Robert placed the letter down on the counter and leaned against the cool granite surface. Where on earth had she gone? Probably to her parents, he thought to himself, immediately believing that he could pull her back from there with a little bit of charm. He pulled his phone from his pocket and pressed Frankie's number, confident that if he played this right, got her parents on-side, she would be home before the day was done.

Frankie drove in silence. She knew Robert would find the note within no more than a few minutes, and then he would call and try and persuade her to come home. As she stared at the road ahead, all she could do was pray her temper would hold, and she would keep calm enough to continue heading north.

The phone sprang to life, and Frankie pressed to accept the call and Robert's voice filled the car.

"What are you doing, Frank? You don't need to do this."

Frankie said nothing in response, waiting to see what he would say next.

"Frank?" pleaded Robert, his fear growing every second that Frankie stayed silent. "Just come home. Talk to your mum. She'll tell you what a huge mistake you're making."

"Mum isn't with me, Robert," said Frankie, finally finding

her voice and somehow sounding far calmer than she felt.

"Oh, so you are there. Frank, this is a joke. You don't need to run to your parent's house. Just come home, and we can talk about it," said Robert, his voice relaxed and friendly, his charm offensive in full flow.

"I'm not coming home."

"Yes, you are. Get your bags and come home. This is silly, Frankie. You can't go and live with your parents. Don't be ridiculous. We need each other. We're good together."

"I'm not going to live with my parents," Frankie replied, unsure whether to tell him exactly where she was going. "I have somewhere to go for a while. It's something I need to do, Robert. For both of us."

"What do you mean you're not going to your parent's house? You can't go and stay with anyone else…." Robert could feel Frankie slipping from his grip, and he began to panic. "Frankie, I need you here with me. This is where you belong. We can work this out; I know we can," he schmoozed down the phone, making Frankie doubt herself for just a second.

"I'm going away to a cottage up north for a while. I need some time to think about what I want."

"North? I don't understand?" Robert was genuinely confused, having entered Frankie's life after Elizabeth had moved in with Frankie's parents and unaware of the home she had left on the North Yorkshire coast.

"There's a place there that I will stay in and do some work on. Just for a while, maybe just a few weeks. I need to do this. It's time I fought a little harder for myself, Robert." There was a clear intent to Frankie's voice that terrified Robert, and he began to realise that Frankie was leaving him, no matter what he said.

"I'm not happy about this, Frankie. I think you're overreacting. And anyway, I can change. I can be better. I really think we can make a go of this if we both try."

Frankie stayed silent for a moment, reflecting on Robert's words and weighing up how best to respond.

"I think that's the point, Robert. I'm not sure you can change or will change, and I'm not sure what you think I need to do differently to stop you from being unfaithful. I want some time alone to think things through. You've done enough damage to our relationship that I think I've earned the right to take a pause and decide if I want to carry on?"

Robert sighed deeply, unable to argue with Frankie's logic. "Okay. So go then. And I'll use the time to think too. Maybe there are things I need to think about, and I'm willing to do it, Frank. But not forever. I want you to come home sooner rather than later, okay? I'll miss you."

"Bye, Robert." Frankie ended the call, and the car fell into silence again.

Frankie switched on the stereo, and the car filled with music as the road stretched ahead. A sudden and welcome feeling of freedom and possibility filled her from head to toe, and she knew that leaving Robert was absolutely the right decision.

Dusk was falling by the time she arrived at the cottage, swinging the car onto the track that led down a steep slope to the cottage driveway. Light streamed from the hotel on the headland already, and there were plenty of cars in the car park. The cottage, in contrast, was in complete darkness and looked about as unwelcoming as Frankie could imagine.

She popped open the door and climbed out of the car, her back screaming at her and her legs heavy and leaden after hours of driving. The air was cold, but the view was outstanding even in the gloom of a winter's afternoon. Frankie could just see down over the fields as they dropped away behind the cottage, with lights from far away houses twinkling in the distance. The sound of waves crashing against the cliffs below was faint but unmistakable. Frankie took a deep breath of the icy cold air and felt it rush into her lungs, and it felt refreshing and cleansing. Although a little scared of what lay ahead, something deep inside her once again confirmed that coming here was the right thing to do.

Picking her way carefully down the path, Frankie dug the key out of her pocket, opened the front door and stepped inside, finding herself in the kitchen. It was small but perfectly configured, with a big oven, a sink that looked out over the fields and lots of worktop space. A large, heavy door opened into the lounge and dining area, with just two comfy looking sofas and a TV at one end and a small dining table and chairs next to a window at the other. Peering through the dirty window, Frankie found she had a clear view of the bay and immediately earmarked one of the four chairs as where she would eat every meal to enjoy that view.

The cottage was all on one level, and up two steps, Frankie discovered a nice sized bathroom, a bedroom with two single beds that she vaguely remembered staying in as a child and then straight ahead of her was the main bedroom. This was a vast room with a large double bed covered in a dust sheet, and there was a big freestanding wardrobe that looked about 100 years old and a chest of drawers nearly the same height as Frankie. But the highlight of the room was a door that opened out onto a small deck that offered uninterrupted views of the bay.

"It is just perfect," Frankie said aloud, surprising herself with the truth of her words.

Frankie fetched the suitcases in from the car, carried them into the bedroom, made up the bed with some bedding she'd brought from home, and ordered herself a pizza after some frantic online searches for nearby takeaways. The biggest challenge in the first hour of residence was finding the plates, knives, and forks, but the cavernous kitchen gave up its secrets soon enough, and the table was set up, ready to eat just as the doorbell rang and the pizza was delivered. Frankie sat down at the table, poured herself a glass of red wine from the box of essentials she'd brought with her and got stuck in, ravenous after her long journey.

Just after 10 pm, Frankie stood and stretched after an evening of watching television. When she switched it off, the cottage suddenly seemed to be so silent that her anxiety spiked a little, and she walked through to the kitchen, opened the front door and took in her surroundings. The proximity of the hotel lit up, and bustling with people made no difference to her feeling of loneliness and isolation. She walked back inside and closed the heavy wooden front door, locking it securely.

Deciding that a hot drink might help her sleep, Frankie boiled the kettle and found a tub of hot chocolate stashed in the cupboard. It was in date which surprised her, the cottage having been vacant since her grandma moved out a decade ago. She made up the hot chocolate, poured a glass of water, turned off the lights, and moved into the lounge. The heating was going off, and the cottage felt chilly, so Frankie turned off all the lights and walked into the bedroom.

The bed looked and smelled welcoming, reminding her of home. She changed into her fleecy pyjamas and climbed under the covers, propping up her pillows to support her head. Relaxing back into them, she held the hot chocolate, blowing it to cool it down and began to reflect on her day. There was no way when she woke in the guest room this morning, Frankie could ever have imagined laying her head on a pillow in a North Yorkshire cottage by tonight. The speed of her departure from the home she shared with Robert was unexpected. Had she done the right thing, she wondered. Robert had sounded regretful and willing to try when she spoke to him earlier, but once again, the nagging sense that it was too little too late was hard to ignore, and she pushed all thoughts of him away.

There was nothing but absolute silence. The cottage was in a small village, one or two other properties within a few metres, but just a track serving them all and presumably leading off towards the farm where the farmer who helped with the cottage lived. Growing up in a busy town and living in Robert's house on a large housing estate meant there was always noise, even at night. Cars were constantly moving through the street, and there was a busy road just half a mile away that never seemed to be empty of traffic. People were coming and going at all hours, and fireworks were often set off at random times of the year and always in the middle of the night. Here there was nothing. Absolute silence. And it was incredible.

Hot chocolate finished, Frankie placed the mug on the bedside table and settled back into the pillows, intending to go to the bathroom in just a moment. But now in bed, warm and cosy and relishing the silence, it became clear the events of the day had exhausted Frankie, and all of the adrenalin that had propelled her through the evening as she unpacked and settled in was gone. Lulled by the warmth, the silence and the emotional and physical exhaustion of the day, Frankie's eyes became heavy and eventually closed. Nevertheless, she had made it through the day, taken the first brave step towards finding herself again, and as she fell asleep, she felt just a little more in control of her life than she had in a very long time.

Chapter 5

Momentarily confused by her location, Frankie quickly realised where she was as she opened her eyes on her first full day in Bayscar. She checked her watch, and it was already 8.45 am! Flopping back down onto the pillow, she realised she had nothing in for breakfast and considered what she could do to feed herself.

A very decadent thought entered her mind - breakfast at the hotel. Given that all she had in the fridge was a couple of left-over slices of pizza and garlic and herb dip, a hearty full English sounded quite appealing. So Frankie leapt out of bed, raced around the cottage, and got herself ready. Steeling herself for the cold, she wrapped warmly in her coat and boots, with a huge scarf looped around her neck.

Pulling the door closed behind her, she set off towards a nearby path and climbed the slope up to the hotel. As she walked, she took in her surroundings, and it was surreal. Vast expanses of fields dotted with sheep on one side and the North Sea for as far as her eye could see on the other. The tide was out, and the beach was an expanse of dark rocks, shiny with seaweed draped over them and pools, shimmering dark grey, reflecting the heavy sky above. Seagulls flew overhead, calling out to each other and evoking memories of childhood holidays to the seaside, past times when Frankie had felt happy and free. Grasses and nettles lined the path, and a brush-like plant she had never seen before, with tiny black seed pods, swayed in the breeze.

There was no one around on this Sunday morning, and Frankie enjoyed the solitude, walking at a pace she felt comfortable with and feeling her calves stretch slightly with the incline of the hill up to the hotel. The hotel was constructed from dark grey stone and had large picture windows that looked out across the bay, and lights twinkled from inside, necessary in the relative darkness of the overcast morning. The car park wasn't as full as when Frankie arrived last night, meaning the chances of getting some breakfast had improved a little more.

Approaching the large oak doors, Frankie removed her scarf and unzipped her coat. Stepping inside, she stepped into a bygone age of wood panelling and patterned carpet. The reception desk was hidden around a corner, and as Frankie walked in, a woman who looked to be in her fifties with hair piled up in a messy bun and a pen poking through it called out, "Hello! Welcome to the Bayscar Hotel. Are you here for breakfast?"

"Good morning," Frankie smiled. "Yes, I'm hoping you can squeeze me in for breakfast. I've just moved into the cottage down the hill, and I have no provisions in yet."

"Ah, you must be Frankie, Elizabeth's granddaughter … it's lovely to meet you. Follow me, and I'll take you through."

Frankie followed the woman, now revealed to be wearing a colourful and floaty dress to compliment the silk scarf draped around her neck, as she made her way down the corridor and then off to the left-hand side and into a spacious restaurant. It was a mystery how the receptionist knew her name, but Frankie was too hungry and distracted by the stunning views from the restaurant windows to worry too much about it.

"Have a lovely breakfast," said the receptionist, smiling warmly and pulling out a chair for Frankie.

"Thank you. I will," replied Frankie, jiggling in her seat, trying to take off her heavy coat, expecting to be left alone to peruse the menu and choose something. But instead, the receptionist wasn't for moving and smiled expectantly.

"I'm Sue, and I run the hotel with my husband, Pete. I'm the receptionist, housekeeper and general dogsbody, and Pete does the bar and the maintenance. We're hoping to be seeing quite a lot of you during your stay."

Frankie smiled back, unsure how to respond. She breathed a sigh of relief when Sue's attention was interrupted by the arrival of another young woman, who walked in and stood for a moment as if appraising the room to establish her next move. She was tall with stunning long dark hair. She looked younger than Frankie, perhaps in her early twenties and seemed effortlessly stylish in her skinny black jeans and t-shirt. Frankie looked down at her checked shirt and jeans, hastily pulled on in her rush to find food without caring how she looked.

"Hi Lilly, darling. Everything's ready for you," said Sue, interrupting Frankie's evaluation of herself against Lilly. "This is Lilly, she's my accountant, well she's everyone's accountant, and she's a little treasure," Sue continued, smiling in Lilly's direction. She then turned to Frankie. "And Lilly, this is Frankie; she's moved into Elizabeth Gleane's cottage; you know the one down the hill."

Frankie felt a little ill at ease, not used to such notoriety. Life in the suburbs of a big town demanded invisibility, heads down, minimal eye contact. Being so central to a conversation between strangers felt uncomfortable, and when added to how hungry Frankie felt, the overall impact was one of intense discomfort.

"So, you're living close to Charlie's farm then? Lucky you," said Lilly, smiling warmly and dazzling Frankie with her perfectly straight teeth.

"Charlie?"

"Yes. Charlie Howard, our local farmer. He looks stern sometimes, but he's a little angel. I'm sure you'll bump into him on your travels."

Frankie was seriously regretting her decision not to buy any groceries on her way up north yesterday. The box of essentials she had so carefully thrown together before she left the house had comprised alcohol and biscuits in the main. When what she really needed was some bread and a couple of bits so she could have had some toast for her breakfast, in the privacy of the cottage.

Lilly seemed more observant than Sue and was quick to spot Frankie's confusion and disquiet, and she began to explain herself. "You're a bit of a celebrity in the village, I'm afraid. I'm quite new to the area, but I know that everyone loved Elizabeth, and no one loved her more than Charlie. He's looked after the cottage since Elizabeth left, and he told me yesterday that your parents had called him and said you were arriving. So, we all knew to expect you and make you feel super welcome!"

"That makes sense then. Thanks for explaining. I was starting to worry there for a minute!" said Frankie, relieved that her parents had smoothed her entrance to the village but still slightly uncomfortable with her lack of invisibility.

"Of course! Anyway, I'm around most days, so why don't we arrange to meet for a drink sometime? Here's my mobile number…." Lilly scribbled her number on an old receipt from her pocket and handed it over. "Text me a couple of dates. Right, I'm off to lose myself in your accounts, Sue. And for goodness' sake, take Frankie's order! She looks about to pass out! Catch you both later!"

After breakfast, Frankie took the same route home and marvelled at how different the bay looked as the light changed. The sky was now peppered with clouds, allowing some of the azure blue above to reflect on the water, creating an almost purple shade to the rockpools littered across the bay as they rippled in the breeze.

Entering the cottage in the full light of day was a pretty different experience from that of the previous evening. Quite unexpectedly, all of the work needed to bring the cottage up to date became crystal clear. The kitchen units were old and needed refurbishment or replacement; the paintwork was tired and peeling, and the floor tiles were chipped. The paintwork was similarly tired in the lounge, and there was a big stain on the ceiling where the roof had leaked last year. The carpet was worn, and a red wine stain was underneath the dining table. The joy of the night was slowly replaced by the panic of the day as the enormity of the task facing her became apparent.

Frankie pulled out her phone and dialled her parents' home number.

Jane answered within two rings. "Oh, my darling. I was about to ring you! How are you getting on?"

"It's okay, Mum. I'm a bit lonely, but I've just been up to the hotel and met some people, and everyone seems nice. I love the cottage, but there's quite a bit to do when you look at it, isn't there?" said Frankie as she walked through the lounge towards the bathroom.

"Yes, darling, but your dad says it's nothing structural, which is good. It just needs refreshing and smartening up," replied Jane.

"I'm not sure my skills extend to replacing a bathroom sink and grouting!" said Frankie, laughing as she took in the mildew and mould forming perfect black outlines to the tiles in the shower enclosure.

"Charlie Howard will help you with anything you can't handle. Your dad called him yesterday afternoon, so he knows you're there, and he'll pop over and say hello once you've settled in a bit. Dad says his number is on the fridge door if you need him."

"Who is this Charlie anyway?" asked Frankie, feeling slightly concerned that this man would be appearing, and she had no idea who he was.

"Oh, he's a lovely young man. A bit older than you and lives on the farm further down the hill from the cottage. His parents were very close to your grandparents, so when the cottage needed caring for, they offered Charlie's services, and it's an arrangement that's just stuck."

"He lives with his mum and dad then?" asked Frankie, feeling slightly better for knowing that she wasn't the only grown adult still relying heavily on their parents in the vicinity.

"Oh no, dear. They moved to Spain about eight years ago left the farm with Charlie. He wasn't too pleased about it then, but he seems to have settled into it now."

Frankie strolled into the bedroom and sat down on the bed, overcome with a wave of tiredness.

"Are you okay, dear?" asked Jane, noticing the long sigh that Frankie let out as she settled.

"Yeah, just tired, I guess. Might be all the fresh sea air?"

"It could be, but let's not forget you've had a rough couple of days. Lots of big emotions, and there's so much to take in. That can wear you out too, you know."

"I know, Mum." Frankie laid her head down on the pillow.

"Why don't you shut your eyes for a bit? The groceries are due to be delivered at noon, so you've some time for a bit of a nap if you want one," said Jane, pleased she had left nothing to chance and sorted out a local delivery to save her daughter trying to find the supermarket on top of everything else.

"That sounds like a good idea, Mum. Love you." Frankie hung up, put her phone down next to her on the bed, and her eyes closed.

When she woke again, the cottage was silent and cold, and Frankie had no idea what to do with herself besides waiting for the groceries. Deciding to tackle the warmth issue first, she turned up the central heating, and the heating system whirred into life. Then she made herself a cup of tea, grabbed the only packet of biscuits in her possession, and settled in the lounge under a heavy and colourful crocheted blanket that her grandma had made. From where she sat, she could see the mist now hanging over the bay and the grey sky reflected in the sea, which matched Frankie's mood perfectly.

She sat for a while, watching the birds flying high in the windy sky, buffeted by the strong breeze coming in off the sea. Then, a text message notification on her phone broke the silence. Digging the phone from her back pocket, Frankie checked the message. It was from Robert.

I miss you so much, Frank. I really think you should come home. Things can be better between us. We just both have to try and be different. I believe we can work, but you need to come home. Rob xx

Frankie stared at the screen, reading the message over and over again. He just doesn't get it, she thought to herself, marvelling at Robert's determination to avoid taking responsibility for the mess of their relationship. He had abused Frankie's trust over and over again, and Frankie had let him do it. Yes, she needed to change, but not how Robert wanted, of that much she was sure.

One line from her grandmother's letter ran through her mind - find someone to cherish you. Frankie tried to shake it off, but it wouldn't budge, repeating itself over again as if forcing Frankie to listen.

"What does that even mean?" Frankie asked, with no one there to answer. "Who even uses the word cherish anymore?"

The cottage remained silent, the call of the seagulls almost mocking Frankie's words. Had she ever felt cherished by Robert? In the last few years, the strongest emotions Frankie could identify were hurt, loneliness and isolation. And she certainly felt lonely and isolated in the cottage, far away from home. But even despite that, going home to Robert was not the answer. As uncomfortable and isolating as being so far away from her parents felt, it was undeniable that going back to Robert now almost guaranteed nothing would change. She would fit back into the humdrum of her life, continue to be lonely and miserable, and Robert would continue to look through Frankie rather than notice the person she was.

Casting the blanket aside and walking to the window, Frankie watched as the waves, tiny as they were at this distance, crashed against the rocks as the tide came back in.

"I'm staying here," she said quietly, her breath creating a mist on the window's glass. The sheep in the field just beyond the garden wall paid no attention, but Frankie didn't care. Somewhere deep inside, a little pool of determination was forming. After years of feeling like a rudderless ship on a stormy sea with no control over where the waves took it, it felt powerful to have even the smallest amount of control at last.

In the early afternoon, groceries - delivered thanks to the foresight of her mum - all packed away and the kitchen bursting with everything she might need, the sun peeked through the clouds, and Frankie looked up from the book she was reading and decided to go for a walk. Pulling the front door closed, she paused for a moment, deciding which direction to take, quickly realising there was a small gate in the wall of her grandma's garden that seemed to allow access to the field. The coastal path was at the other side of the field, so Frankie set off into the garden, through the gate, and into the muddy field beyond.

Progress was slow, the joy of her surroundings and the icy cold air in her lungs doing nothing to improve her speed with such a steep decline and rough terrain. But she was determined to get herself to the coastal path. She picked her way down the field, failing to realise that the gate she needed to access the path was blocked by a large number of very muddy sheep. As she approached them, her heart sank. Any hope of them moving out of courtesy evaporated instantly, and the sheep simply stood and stared at her without interest. Unable to accept defeat and determined not to go back to the cottage without so much as setting foot on the path, Frankie began to wave her arms around to scare them into moving.

"Come on! Shoo! Move!" she called, eliciting no response from the flock.

A few minutes of wild gesticulation and encouragement did nothing to move the sheep, and Frankie was about to grudgingly admit defeat when the sound of an engine drew her attention. In the distance, at the top of the hill, a white flatbed truck was moving in her direction, and at some speed. Pulling alongside her, the truck stopped, and a man stepped out.

"What do you think you're doing?" he asked without introduction.

"Oh. I'm trying to get to the gate," said Frankie, incredulous at the question and the somewhat obvious answer.

"If you shout at the sheep, you'll scare them. They are nervous animals. Can't you just use the other gate instead?"

"What other gate?" Having lived in the cottage for less than 24 hours, the fact Frankie was aware of even one gate felt like an achievement.

The man rolled his eyes in irritation and pointed to the other end of the field. "That gate."

"I didn't see it. Sorry. I only arrived yesterday," explained Frankie indignantly. "Sorry if I scared your sheep." She looked at the man and took in his muddy clothes and boots, all very much in keeping with his farming profession, she noted.

"If you arrived yesterday, are you Elizabeth's granddaughter?" the farmer asked, his face softening slightly.

"I am," Frankie replied. "My name is Frankie. And you are?"

"Sorry, I should have introduced myself sooner. I'm Charlie Howard. I look after the cottage. Nice to meet you." He stepped forward, wiped his hand on his jeans and thrust it forward to shake Frankie's.

"Ah, so you're Charlie. Nice to meet you too," said Frankie, surprised by both his age and the surliness of his initial approach. She had been expecting an older man, and certainly someone far more polite and welcoming. Lilly said he was an angel, but he seemed far more grumpy than angelic.

"How are you finding the cottage? Everything okay?"

"Yes, it's fine, thank you. Although I've not been in there long, so it's early days."

"Well, if you need anything, just give me a call, okay? My number is on the fridge door. I can help you with anything you need," Charlie replied, smiling at last. "Do you want me to move these sheep for you? I imagine you're more comfortable in a town than a field."

"That would be helpful," Frankie replied, ignoring his sarcasm.

Charlie walked up to the sheep, and they immediately scattered, clearing a path to the gate. Frankie walked over to it and let herself through. "Thanks for that."

"You're welcome. Enjoy your walk," Charlie called over the fence, watching her as she walked away.

Frankie waved and continued to walk until she found a bench that overlooked the bay. She sat down, her body humming with energy after the exertion of crossing the field and the interaction with Charlie. The view was exquisite, and the sound of the waves hitting the rocks below was clear and soothing. Her mind wandered gently as she listened to nature, the birds calling, the sea crashing into the shore and the wind blowing through the trees perched high on the cliff, and a sense of stillness descended upon her. For a few moments, the burden of her decision and the state of her relationship melted away, and Frankie was at peace. A sense of hope and possibility was building, and Frankie was already feeling much more like her old self.

Chapter 6

The first few days in Bayscar passed in a complex mix of old and new circumstances as Frankie navigated around the cottage, the village, and her much changed living arrangements. However, she realised that the most challenging aspect of this relocation was the lack of human contact and conversation. Frankie was only too aware of how lonely she used to feel with Robert; he was rarely home. But the absolute isolation of the cottage provided a silence that far surpassed anything she had experienced with Robert. Surprisingly, the job she had hated when she lived down south suddenly became her lifeline.

Frankie spent much of each day on the phone, having the same conversation about home improvements repeatedly, marvelling at the varied ways people had for telling her they weren't interested. Some people were polite and explained carefully that they were about to hang up. At the opposite end of the politeness spectrum, others simply yelled expletives before angrily ending the call. Occasionally, she would find herself caught on the phone with someone who was lonely, most often elderly, and oddly, those were the calls Frankie now enjoyed the most.

Apart from her work, she took solace in the beauty of the nature around her and made herself get out for walks as often as she could. However, she rarely walked around the village itself, preferring the solitude of the coastal path. For someone who was quite lonely, Frankie knew she was avoiding face-to-face contact with anyone who might be interested or nosey, enough to ask about her life.

Jane had pointed out that Frankie was avoiding people and needed to pull herself together to get her life moving. And despite her frequent denials, Frankie knew Jane was right. She just needed something or someone to nudge her into action.

Saturday rolled around once again, marking a whole week since Frankie had left Robert, and joyful at the prospect of a weekend free of home improvement calls, Frankie had risen early and decided to go out and watch the sunrise from her favourite spot on the coastal path. Wrapping herself up as warmly as possible against the bitingly cold January winds, she set off through the gate and across Charlie's field, passing the flock of sheep still huddled together and sleeping alongside the shelter of a hedge.

She closed the field gate and headed off towards the bench, 200 yards up ahead. From there, she could see across to the other side of the bay and all of the tiny villages dotted along its edge, snaking down the cliff face towards the sea. The wind stung Frankie's cheeks as she sat down and waited for the sun to appear on the horizon, and she held her gloved hands against her face to warm her skin.

As the sun rose, the sky erupted into a stunning array of orange in every shade, the water mirroring the sky. The colours shifted and changed as the sun continued its climb, the clouds streaking across the sky in shades of lilac and dark orange. It was exquisite, and Frankie was transfixed, moved by the grandeur and power of nature in all its glory.

Frankie watched until the sun was lost in the clouds as it

climbed, swallowed by the heavy grey shroud that filled the sky as far as the eye could see. She had lost all sense of time and was deep in thought, enjoying the tranquillity of her surroundings. But a flock of seagulls rose from the cliffs below and startled her, instantly drawing her attention to the chill in her bones and, more importantly, the heavy cold raindrops that were starting to fall.

Realising she was at least fifteen minutes' walk from any form of shelter, Frankie scoured the area for the best route back to the cottage. She stood and looked up at the network of paths, still unfamiliar enough that she had to think about a route home. She spotted a trail that followed a tree line and decided that the shelter the trees offered was probably her best bet, the rain gathering pace with every passing minute. She bolted in the direction of the trees and followed the path up the hill towards the hotel.

Before she reached the hotel, Frankie took a path off to the right and ran as fast as she could towards the bus stop shelter on the corner near the tea shop and post office. She couldn't face going into the hotel, especially looking like a drowned rat. The bus stop provided shelter, and Frankie sat down, grateful for the seat and to be out of the rain. When she had left the cottage, the village was deserted, but a few people were now milling around, hidden under their umbrellas. One or two cars drove past, and Frankie checked her watch. To her surprise, it was almost 9 am. Somehow, she had spent over two hours on the bench, staring out to sea. No wonder she was so cold!

The rain started coming down more heavily, and Frankie needed to get home, quickly realising that she would get very wet in the process. She was about to stand up when someone ran into the bus shelter and shook the water from their jacket.

"Hello, you!"

Frankie looked up at Lilly's beaming face and smiled back

warmly. "Hello! You look as wet as me!"

"I am drenched. The weather wasn't too bad when I set off, but that's Yorkshire for you. Expect the unexpected when it comes to the weather! What are you doing out this early?"

"I went to watch the sun come up, and lost track of time. And you?" Frankie asked although the answer was pretty obvious based on Lilly's trainers and leggings.

"I try and go for a jog three to four mornings a week. Burn off all the nervous energy that builds up from living somewhere so quiet!"

"Yeah, it certainly is quiet," agreed Frankie. "But I quite like that."

"It has its advantages, I'll give you that," replied Lilly enigmatically, looking across at the teashop as the owner switched on the lights and flipped the sign to 'open'. "Do you fancy grabbing coffee and a pastry as we never got around to arranging to meet up?"

Frankie's immediate reaction was to say no, but something about Lilly's smile made her change her mind. That, and the prospect of a freshly baked muffin and a hot cup of coffee. "I'd love to."

"Right. In that case, let's run!" cried Lilly, and she sprinted off across the road, leaving Frankie to follow behind, slightly less nimble in her winter coat and walking boots.

The teashop was everything a quaint village teashop should be, with a bell that chimed as you walked in, gingham table cloths, dried flowers in jugs dotted around and of course, an incredible view out across the bay. Or at least, what would have been a fantastic view across the bay if a thick fog hadn't completely obscured it as it rolled in from the North Sea.

"What can I get you dears?" asked a small, kindly faced woman, pen in hand and note pad at the ready.

"Hi, Rose. This is Frankie. She's moved into Elizabeth's cottage," said Lilly, beaming from Rose to Frankie.

"Hi," said Frankie shyly. It still felt odd to be so well-known by strangers.

"Hello, my dear! I heard you were here. Susan mentioned it when she came over from some eggs on Thursday last. She'd run out at the hotel. We do what we can to help each other, you know. Your grandmother was quite a lady. We were all very sorry to hear she'd passed on. Very sad news indeed."

Frankie didn't quite know how to respond without crying and settled on a simple, "Thank you. I miss her very much."

Lilly watched Frankie wrestle with her emotions and decided to take control. "I'll have a cappuccino and two almond croissants, please, Rose. Frankie?"

"Cappuccino and a muffin if you have any?" Frankie replied, grateful to Lilly for bringing the discussion about her grandma to a close.

"I've got blueberry, chocolate or banana, my dear. What do you fancy?"

"The banana muffins are to die for if that helps?" said Lilly, winking at Frankie.

"How can I ignore a recommendation like that? I'll go for banana, please, Rose."

"Okay, dears, give me five minutes," said Rose, as she turned and walked away.

"So, how's your first week been?" asked Lilly, taking off her wet jacket and draping it on the chair behind her.

Frankie unzipped her coat and used the time it took to take it off and hang it behind her to frame her response.

"It's been okay. I've been working all week, but I've tried to get out every day for a walk when the weather has allowed me to."

"If there's one thing we have an abundance of in Bayscar,

its places to walk! What do you do then? To be able to work from here, I mean?"

Frankie explained her job to Lilly, sharing some of the funnier experiences over the years and playing down the fact she hated it with a passion. Then, in turn, Lilly explained that she was an accountant. She had moved from Harrogate to Bayscar just a little under two years ago, picking up work with the hotel as their accountant and then slowly building up her business doing the accounts for small businesses in the village.

"Here you go, my dears. That should warm you up a bit," said Rose as she placed the steaming cappuccinos down on the table and then laid the muffin and croissants down with knives and napkins. "If you need anything else, just shout. I'm in the back baking some cookies, but I'll hear you."

The women fell into silence as they tucked into their breakfast, and Frankie knew within one bite that Lilly's taste in muffins was excellent. Rose bustled in and out each time the door chimed, and more people walked in, taking shelter from the rain. Soon the teashop was packed, and Rose was rushed off her feet.

"Hello, Lil! I didn't see you when I walked in!" cried a voice from the next table. Lilly looked up from her croissant and beamed.

"Hey, Tash! How are you? This is Frankie. She's living in Elizabeth's cottage down the hill."

"Hi," said Frankie, smiling shyly.

"Good to meet you!" said Tash, grinning. "Your Nan was my Sunday school teacher when I was at primary school. I loved her. She was a sweetheart. Can't believe she's gone."

Franke was hit with another wave of grief and nodded gratefully at Tash before focussing on her coffee and willing the tears not to fall.

Once again, Lilly stepped in and struck up a conversation

with Tash, leaving Frankie to gather herself, picking at the crumbs left by her muffin and regretting having only ordered one. The teashop was buzzing with people, and it was blissfully warm and cosy. Unfortunately, the mist had rolled into the village now, and there was no hint of any coastline visible across the street. Even the bus shelter she had sat in just half an hour ago disappeared from view.

As everyone around her chatted away happily, Frankie watched and marvelled at how much her life had changed in such a short space of time. And better still, she was enjoying the change. Of course, it was uncomfortable and pushed her outside of her comfort zone, but it also felt amazing to be so free, surrounded by so much life and such breathtaking nature. There was such potential in the village; so much warmth and personality.

"So, are you married, Frankie?" asked Tash, ripping Frankie from her thoughts and dragging her back to the conversation.

"Me? No. Never. I mean, no, not yet." Frankie winced at how she sounded, but the question had thrown her. "You?" she asked Tash, keen to deflect.

"Oh, that's such a pity. Not found the right man yet, eh? I've been married for eight years in June. Two kids, three dogs. Living the dream, you know!" Tash laughed.

"Wow! Eight years is some achievement. How old are your children?" Frankie asked, ignoring Tash's apparent sympathy.

"Emma is five, and Aiden is two next week. I'd love to say they're little angels, but I'd be lying. They drive me mad half the time. The other half the time, they're asleep!" Tash laughed again, and Frankie smiled.

"Can I get you anything else, dears?" asked Rose, as she rotated around the tables collecting orders.

"Can I get another muffin?" Frankie asked, surprising herself with her devil-may-care attitude to weight gain.

"Of course, dear. And another coffee?"

Frankie nodded and watched as Lilly ordered another coffee and wrestled with her conscience about having a banana muffin too. It wasn't much of a wrestle, though, and Rose scribbled the muffin order down as she walked away.

Frankie sat listening to the conversations humming around her, still not confident to begin one of her own and waiting to be invited in.

"....so I said to him, Charlie if your wife asked you to do it, you should!" said Tash, deep in conversation with the woman sitting opposite her.

"And what did he say to that?" asked the woman.

"He said he would think about it but that he wasn't comfortable with the idea. But, honestly, Bev, he is so stubborn, he drives me mad!"

Rose appeared with the muffins and fresh coffee, and Frankie and Lilly once again focussed on their food, looking up to smile as Tash and Bev continued their dissection of village life.

"So, what about you?" Frankie asked Lilly, between mouthfuls. "Why did you move here from Harrogate? I imagine the pace here is a fair bit slower!"

Lilly took a bite of her muffin and then a sip of her coffee. "I needed to get away for a bit, you know—family stuff. I fancied living by the sea, and there was a nice flat to rent above the butchers, round the corner. So, I left. It's not a big deal. I like it here."

Frankie didn't know Lilly at all, but even she could tell that there was more to the story than Lilly was letting on. She looked ill at ease for the first time since they'd met.

"It seems Bayscar is a place where people come if they need to get away then." Frankie knew as soon as she'd said it that it opened up questions she didn't want to answer, but it was too late.

"Oh, so are you here to get away from something too?"

"I guess so," Frankie replied, observing Lilly and judging whether she should be honest. It felt too raw to share, yet she wanted to say something. "I needed some space, you know, to think things through. Decide what I want out of life? And Grandma left me the keys to her cottage. So here I am."

"Here we both are," said Lilly, raising her coffee cup and clinking it with Frankie's. "Here's to escaping to Bayscar and finding new friends."

"I'll drink to that."

Chapter 7

A cargo ship sailed across the horizon, and Frankie watched its slow progress as she worked her way through her calls for the afternoon. Looking out to sea had become a welcome distraction as she ploughed through her daily workload. The constant motion and changing colours reflected the sky above, mesmerising her and soothing her stress levels like nothing before. In fact, her connection to the sea was growing with each passing day, and it was beginning to occur to Frankie that going back down south and moving away from the coast would be much more challenging than she had ever imagined when she arrived a few weeks ago.

Since the morning in the teashop, Lilly had been around to visit the cottage and even helped Frankie paint the kitchen just last weekend. It was no longer a peeling magnolia wreck and was now a fresh sunshine yellow, and every time Frankie walked in there, she felt joyful. They had painted all day and then crashed in front of the TV and watched an old black and white movie on channel 5 with a Chinese takeaway and a couple of bottles of wine.

Lilly was still cautious about sharing too much of her life before Bayscar, but Frankie didn't mind, having equal hesitation in sharing the details of her relationship with Robert. Whenever she considered telling Lilly anything about him or their time together, it seemed to hammer home the humiliation and hurt his behaviour had generated. She wasn't ready to face that yet, and Lilly didn't press for more information. It wasn't uncomfortable, and they both seemed to share a sense that their past lives were unimportant; it was time to start looking forward and toast the opportunities the future afforded them both.

Despite his offer to pop around, there had been no sign of Charlie thus far, and he frustratingly remained an enigma for Frankie, a mystery figure, a grumpy angel, someone that everyone except her knew and loved. Lilly never stopped singing his praises, and Charlie somehow seemed to be involved in every aspect of the villagers' lives except Frankie's. But after his attitude in the field on her first day, Frankie was in no rush to call him up and ask for his help with anything.

Finishing her final call of the day, Frankie stood and stretched, her back aching after two hours of sitting in the wooden chair. Checking her watch, she realised it was time to turn the oven on for dinner, a re-heated beef stew leftover from two nights ago. With the novelty of constant takeaways now very much worn off, home cooking was the order of the day and a quick trip into town to fill up the fridge and freezer was all it took to set Frankie on the path to wholesome and nutritious meals once more.

Oven on and stew removed from the fridge, Frankie opened the heavy door into the lounge and began to tidy away her work things for the day. She looked up and saw the cargo ship as it disappeared behind the headland on the other side of the bay, and then her phone rang.

"Hello?"

"Hi, Frankie. It's Simon." Her boss never rang her, and Frankie immediately began to panic.

"Hi, Simon. Is everything okay?"

"How are things up in the wilds of Yorkshire? Are you all settled in?" he asked, trying to avoid the question which had prompted the call in the first place. This was to be no social chit chat.

"Yes, I'm fine. It's fine. I love it here," Frankie replied, knowing she sounded agitated, mainly because she felt agitated.

"Good. That's excellent. Well, the thing is, Frankie, I've been going through your figures for the last quarter and well, to put it bluntly, they're awful."

Frankie knew it had been a bad quarter but who the hell buys home improvements in winter after a worldwide pandemic?

"…so I'm afraid we'll have to let you go. I'm sorry, Frankie. We just can't keep on carrying you."

The room began to spin, and Frankie sat down on the settee, hoping to figure out a suitable response. But she had nothing. She hated the job. She only did it for the money. But she wouldn't beg. No way.

"Frankie?" Simon pressed, unnerved by her silence.

"Fine."

"What?"

"I said fine. Thank you for letting me know," she said tersely.

"We'll pay you until the end of the month."

"Whatever. Thanks, Simon." She hung up, walked into the kitchen, turned off the oven, grabbed her keys and walked out of the cottage.

Mid-February meant the evenings were getting lighter, and Frankie was grateful because the only place she wanted to be right now was as far away from that phone call as she could get. She needed to be by the sea; she wanted to feel cold, ice cold. So, she took the quickest route to the coastal path, cutting through the golf course next to the hotel, down through the tree line and past Charlie's field.

Once at the cliff edge, she stood, staring out to sea, and the tears finally began to fall. She didn't know what she was crying about - the job? No, she hated the job. Was it the money? Probably. She had no way to support herself without the pittance she earned. But the tears were bigger than that; the sobs were more heart-rending. The emotion that poured out was like a tsunami of grief and anger for everything she had lost. Her grandma, her relationship, her home and now her job. What else was left to be wrenched away from her?

Her body shook with the force of the tears as the wind blew hard into her face, stinging her cheeks and making her shake violently with cold.

Up on the hill, Charlie was driving through his fields, checking the livestock, when he noticed someone standing far too close to the cliff edge. Concerned, he drove as close to the coastal path as he was able and then, leaving his truck behind, he jumped the fence. Running down the path, the figure grew closer, and he could see long hair blowing in the wind with no sign of any coat. Whoever it was would be freezing, and by the way they were stood, there was no way Charlie could walk away. This looked very much like a person in trouble.

As he approached, he recognised Frankie and his heart lifted a little. At least it was someone he knew. That would make it easier to talk her down from whatever she was thinking of doing. He walked towards her slowly, weighing his options and trying to form the best approach.

"Hey? Are you okay?" he called, hoping the wind wouldn't carry his voice in the wrong direction, a strong breeze blowing in from the sea.

Frankie looked around but didn't respond.

"Frankie? Are you okay?" he tried again, not taking his eyes off her and noticing her body shaking with sobs as he got ever closer.

He continued to approach, and when he was within touching distance, he tried once more.

"Frankie, will you take my jacket? You must be so cold? Here…" he pulled off his jacket and wrapped it around her shoulders, and to his relief, she didn't resist.

"Come away from the edge, okay? It's not safe," he said softly, holding her shoulders and easing her backwards. She moved as instructed, and he managed to get her away from the edge and over to the bench he had seen her sit on so many times these last few weeks.

They sat in silence for a few minutes, Frankie crying softly and Charlie unable to fathom what he should do next. Finally, he settled on practicality.

"It's too cold to be out here without a jacket. Can I take you home?"

Frankie nodded, her face streaked with tears and her whole body shivering in the cold air. The light was fading, and Charlie knew he needed to make her move soon, so he eased her up, and they began the slow walk back to the gate that led up to the cottage garden. They walked in silence. Frankie had stopped crying, meaning Charlie could relax just a little. She was so small and fragile compared to his height and build. At six foot four, he often found himself the tallest in the room, and next to Frankie, he felt like a giant. He placed his arm around her tiny shoulders and pulled her against him for heat, and she didn't resist.

When they got to the cottage, Frankie handed Charlie the key, and he opened the door, her hands too shaky to do it herself. She walked in, and he followed, keen to make sure she was okay to be left alone. He considered calling Lilly, but he knew she was in Harrogate trying to talk to her parents this afternoon, and she would have enough on her plate. So, for now, he would try and help Frankie himself.

Frankie settled on the settee, and Charlie spotted Elizabeth's large crochet blanket, which he placed over her legs. Without asking, he walked through the cottage to the spare bedroom and pulled the extra duvet down from the top of the wardrobe. Taking it from its protective bag, he opened it up, shook it to fluff the inside, and then returned to Frankie and placed it carefully over her legs. She was still shaking, and he was concerned, so he went to the kitchen, turned up the heating, filled the kettle, set it to boil, and then spotting the stew on the worktop, switched on the oven. A few minutes later, the stew was in the oven, the cottage was beginning to warm up, and he returned to Frankie's side with two cups of coffee.

"I wasn't sure if you took sugar?" he said as he placed the coffee down on the table next to Frankie. She shook her head and smiled slightly.

Charlie sat next to her and rested his coffee on his thigh, running his left hand around the rim absentmindedly as he tried to figure out what to do next. His wedding ring glinted in the lamplight, catching Frankie's eye, and she remembered Tash talking about his wife in the teashop.

"Thank you," she whispered. "I'm sorry I scared you."

Relieved to hear her speak, at last, Charlie turned and smiled at Frankie kindly.

"I'm just sorry you were so upset," he replied, meaning every word. She looked so broken, he wanted to help somehow, but he had no idea what was wrong. "Is there anything I can do to help? Anything you need?"

"You've done enough. I don't know what happened, honestly. I think I just lost it. It's been such a terrible few weeks...." She trailed off, and the crying started again.

"You must miss your grandma terribly. I know we all do,

and we barely knew her compared to you. I hear you were very close?"

Frankie nodded.

"Is there anything else troubling you? I want to help you if I can...."

Frankie looked at him and saw the kindness in his grey eyes, his face creased in concern, and all at once, she realised what a terrible fright she must have given him, standing there, on the edge, looking like she was about to do something awful. She knew he deserved some kind of explanation.

"I lost my job. It was all I had left. I've lost everything else: my home, my relationship. I walked away from it all to come here and find myself. And now I'm unemployed. I've made such a mess of everything." She had no idea why she was telling Charlie the truth about her situation after having kept it a secret from everyone since she got there, but something about him felt safe.

Charlie listened as she spoke, taking in the snippets of her life she was sharing, his mind working furiously to figure out how he could help her. He watched as she reached up and moved some strands of her dark blond hair out of her face, her green eyes shining with tears yet to fall. Freckles dusted her face, and in that moment, he was struck by how beautiful she was.

Disappointed at himself for such a hugely inappropriate thought, he tried to focus on the quest for some kind of assistance for Frankie. He quickly remembered a conversation he'd had with Pete at the hotel two nights ago.

"There's a job going at the hotel. Waitressing, I think. I could put in a good word for you with Pete and Sue, although I imagine they'd be happy to consider you."

Frankie smiled and nodded. "That would be great if you could. Maybe we could walk up there together when you have time? I don't want to be any bother."

"It wouldn't be any bother at all, honestly. They need the help, you need a job, and I am more than happy to be the one that links you all together. We can go up tomorrow if you're up to it?"

"I will be. Thank you, Charlie. Not just for the job thing, but for, you know, finding me and bringing me home." Frankie was more grateful than she could express. It had been so foolish to walk out without a coat in this weather and in such an emotional state.

"Will you stay for dinner? I have plenty…." The smell of the stew was beginning to permeate into the living room.

"I'd love to, but I…."

"Oh, my goodness, I'm sorry!" cried Frankie, remembering he was married, and his wife would be waiting for him at home. "I shouldn't have asked!"

"No, it's fine. Asking was lovely. I just need to get back and finish what I was doing when I saw you, that's all. Maybe another time?"

Frankie was confused, but Charlie stood, and the moment was lost.

"Don't get up; I'll see myself out. My number is on the fridge, okay, so if you need anything, make sure you call me please?"

Frankie nodded obediently.

"I'll come by and pick you up at noon tomorrow, and we'll walk up and see Pete and Sue - unless you're not up to it. Let me know, okay?"

"Okay. Thanks, Charlie. I mean it. I'm so grateful you found me."

"So am I. Now keep warm, enjoy your stew, and I'll see you tomorrow."

And with that, he disappeared into the kitchen, and Frankie listened as he pulled the front door closed behind him.

Frankie looked up at the ceiling. "Maybe he is an angel, after all, Grandma."

Chapter 8

The morning passed in a flurry of housework and nervous energy. Meeting Pete and Sue to talk about the waitressing job would be the closest thing to an interview Frankie could recall in years. The very idea made her feel jittery and on edge, but by the time noon arrived, the cottage looked tidy and cleaner than it had in a decade.

A man of his word, Charlie knocked on the front door at midday, and when Frankie opened the door, he couldn't quite believe his eyes. Having only seen her in jeans and jumpers, heavy coat and boots, the sight of Frankie in a dress was surprisingly wonderful.

"Come in for a sec. I need to get my shoes on, and I'll be ready," Frankie said, closing the door and scampering past in stockinged feet and rushing to the bedroom.

"There's no rush. I told Pete to expect us by quarter past anyway," Charlie called out, hoping his voice would carry to the other end of the long narrow cottage, before sitting down and taking in how much more organised and tidy the room looked compared to the previous evening. The pile of papers and folders on the table had disappeared, presumably no longer required due to the sudden change in employment status. And the whole room just seemed to look and smell loved for the first time since Elizabeth had left.

"Okay, I'm ready," said Frankie, stepping into the room smiling. "How do I look?"

"You look...." Charlie paused, trying to work out what to say. She looked beautiful, but he couldn't say that. "You look very nice. Very professional. I'm sure Pete and Sue will appreciate the effort."

"Thanks. I really need this job, so I want to make a good impression."

"Well, I think you're guaranteed to do that," he replied, looking away to avoid eye contact. Frankie was unsettling him, and it didn't feel good. "Come on. Let's go and get you employed."

The walk up to the hotel took no more than five minutes, and before Frankie knew it, she was walking through the big oak doors and taking off her heavy coat, while Charlie went into the office to find Pete. She felt sick with nerves and took a couple of deep breaths to calm herself. It was so important this went well, the alternative being a call to her parents to ask for money. And anything would be better than that.

"Frankie! Good to see you. I'm Pete." Bald and a few inches shorter than Charlie, Pete Rodney seemed genuinely happy to meet Frankie, and her confidence lifted just a fraction. He wore black jeans and a checked shirt, and there was a twinkle in his eye that made Frankie feel at ease somehow.

"It's lovely to meet you too. Thank you for seeing me. I really appreciate it."

"It's no trouble at all. You'd be doing us a big favour if this works out. Amelie left at short notice, and we need to fill the role as quickly as possible. No time to advertise. Follow me." Pete marched off in the direction of the office, and Frankie looked at Charlie nervously.

"Go on. You'll be fine. They'll love you."

"Okay. Will you be here when I come out?" Frankie asked, immediately regretting how needy she sounded.

"I'll be in the bar. Now go!" Charlie smiled and waved his hand in the direction of Pete's retreating figure, leaving Frankie with no option but to face the interview with as much confidence as she could muster.

Twenty minutes later, a beaming Frankie walked into the bar and sat down on the stool next to Charlie.

"I got the job!"

"I thought you would. They would have been crazy to let you walk out of here. I think you'll be a great waitress," Charlie said smiling, pleased that his attempt to help Frankie had worked out so well. "When do you start?"

"Thursday evening. Apparently, it's usually a quiet night and a good chance for me to learn the ropes. They need me to be up to speed by Friday if possible." Frankie was nervous; the learning curve would be steep, for sure. But this was a job she knew she could do, and more importantly, it was a way for her to earn money and be independent. It wouldn't be enough money, but it was a start. "Thank you so much, Charlie. I know you put in a good word for me with Sue."

"I just told her I thought you'd be great with the customers; friendly and approachable." As he spoke, Charlie watched Frankie gazing around the bar and through to the restaurant beyond; her eyes wide with curiosity. She looked so full of joy and possibility; Charlie was transfixed.

"What are you two up to then?" Lilly appeared at Charlie's side, forcing him to tear his eyes away from Frankie, breaking the spell. And he was grateful.

"Frankie? Do you want to tell Lilly the good news?" he asked playfully as Lilly pulled up a stool, happy to be out of the dingy office where she had been hidden all morning working through the stack of receipts and invoices that Pete had pulled together for the last month.

"Oh yes! Guess what? I've got a job here. As a waitress! I start on Thursday!"

"I thought you were working for that home improvement place?" Lilly asked, confused and out of step with the last 24 hours.

"They let me go yesterday. So, Charlie helped me get a job here. Isn't that amazing?"

"It's completely amazing. Congratulations. You hated that cold-calling gig anyway, right? So, this is a total win for you. I'm really pleased, Frankie. And Charlie, how very nice of you to step in and rescue a damsel in distress! Not like you at all, eh?" said Lilly in a gently mocking tone and eliciting a broad smile from Charlie.

"I do what I can when I can, that's all. It's not a big deal," he replied, keen to minimise any focus on him.

"Well, it's a big deal to me, Charlie," said Frankie, touching his arm gently. "I am so grateful, honestly. You saved me yesterday."

"Charlie is a wonder to us all. We'd be lost without him," said Lilly, reaching her arm around his shoulder and hugging him.

Frankie took in the scene as Charlie leaned in, and Lilly squeezed him tightly. They were close - far closer than Frankie had realised.

Thursday evening came around in a flash, and at 5.30, Frankie pulled her front door closed and walked nervously up to the hotel. She was wearing the required black skirt and a white blouse, both of which she had brought with her by some unimaginable fluke! The wind was brisk, and even though bulbs were peeking through the ground as the first sign of spring, there was still an icy bite to the breeze as it whipped around Frankie's legs.

The hotel was warm, and the restaurant looked quite full

to Frankie's horror. Having been assured that Thursdays were always quiet, the sight of almost every table being occupied left Frankie feeling even more nervous than before she'd arrived.

She was quickly partnered up with Byron, a young man, perhaps late teens, who had been working at the hotel since he was 14. Now one of the hotel's most experienced waiting staff, Byron wasted no time taking Frankie under his wing and showing her the ropes. It was surprisingly straightforward. Contrary to the slightly dated interior, Pete had invested in tablets for the evening service, with menus preloaded and orders sent straight to a screen in the kitchen. All Frankie needed to do was listen, tap and collect the food when her tablet beeped to say the order was ready. Compared to a brief stint working at her Uncle Patrick's restaurant in Dublin almost twenty years ago, with notepads, pens and angry chefs waving pieces of paper around, it was simplicity itself.

The shift passed quickly, and by 9.30, the tables started to clear, and Byron showed her how to set everything up for breakfast. Frankie's confidence began to creep up as each table left, calling their thanks and appreciation over their shoulders. And it felt good.

"Here's your share of the tips," said Byron, handing over a small brown envelope. "You did well tonight. You're a natural! See you tomorrow." He walked over to the bar area where a woman, presumably his mother, ruffled his hair and led him out to the car park.

Frankie opened the envelope and smiled at the collection of notes and coins it contained. She had done an excellent job, and this proved it.

"You look exhausted, Frankie! But my goodness me, you've done well tonight. You've taken to this like a duck to water!" said Sue, resplendent in a floaty red chiffon skirt and white ruffled blouse. "Thank goodness Charlie sent you to talk to us!"

"Thanks, Sue. I enjoyed it, to be honest. I am tired out, though. Not used to being on my feet for so long!" Frankie sat down, and Sue followed her lead, taking a seat at a nearby table. "I am so grateful to Charlie for this. He seems like a nice man. Kind."

"Oh, he is. Charlie is one of life's real diamonds. He would do anything for anyone that man and never ask for a thing in return. It's so sad what happened, but he seems to be moving on at last."

Frankie was intrigued. "What did happen, if you don't mind me asking? Unless you'd rather not say...."

"Oh, no. Don't be silly. It's no secret. Coming up for three years ago, Charlie lost his wife to cancer. It was heart-breaking for the whole village. She was such a wonderful girl, a real angel. Her name was Katie, and they'd been together for years, bless them, but only married less than six months when she got ill. It broke his heart; it broke everyone's heart. It was a tragedy." Sue dabbed a tear from her eye and sighed deeply.

Frankie was struck dumb. She had no idea! A strong instinct to look after Charlie rose in her chest, but she pushed it away. It wasn't her place. They were barely friends.

"That's so sad," she finally whispered, although aware of how inadequate it sounded.

"It is, dear. But time moves on, and we all have to move with it, I'm afraid. It's taken Charlie a long time to smile again, but I think he's starting to heal. Seems a bit more cheerful these last few months. Fingers crossed, eh? He's a good man; he deserves to be happy again. Right. Come on, you. Let's get you off home. You've another shift tomorrow night, and I need you fresh and raring to go!"

Both women stood, and Frankie followed Sue out of the

restaurant and into the bar and there, nursing a pint in what was presumably his usual spot, was Charlie.

"How'd she do, then?" he asked Sue cheekily.

"She did just fine, Charlie, as we knew she would." Sue ruffled his blond hair as she walked past him and towards the reception.

"You look exhausted," he said to Frankie, smiling.

"You're the second person to tell me that in the last five minutes. I can take a hint. I'm going home."

"Can I walk with you? If you don't mind?" Charlie asked, standing up and pulling on his jacket.

Slightly taken by surprise but happy to have some company walking down the dark track to the cottage, Frankie nodded and grabbed her coat from behind the bar.

The sky was clear, the moon and stars breath-taking in their clarity. As Frankie and Charlie stepped through the oak doors and into the night air, their breath clouded in front of them, a light frost glimmering in the moonlight on the grass to their left. They walked through the car park without saying a word and turned right to go down the track. The silence was unnerving, and in the end, Frankie couldn't bear it.

"Thank you so much for helping me get the job. Honestly, I really appreciate it. You literally saved me yesterday," she said, surprising herself with the honesty of her words.

"It's nothing. I would have done that for anyone. You needed help, and I happened to be there. I'm just glad I could help as much as I did."

"I'm starting to realise how much everyone in the village relies on you. I don't think I've ever met someone that helps so many people…."

"It's just nice to give something back. This village helped me when I needed it most. The least I can do is reciprocate where I can."

"Well, I think it's lovely that everyone here is kind and generous. It's nothing like where I come from. No-one knows anyone; there's no community at all." Frankie thought back to Robert's house and the cul-de-sac. She didn't even know most of the people that lived there. Houses just yards from her own, and yet rarely was there any contact at all, let alone any support. Not like Bayscar.

"Without this community, I would never have survived losing Katie. Sue and Pete were incredible. They picked me up and put me back together." Charlie stopped walking and kicked a stone, jamming his hands in his pockets. "Katie was my wife...."

"I know," Frankie said quickly, wanting to prevent Charlie from sharing anything he didn't want to. "Sue told me what happened. I'm so sorry, Charlie."

They looked at each other for a moment, and then Charlie began walking again, head down.

"She had breast cancer, and it spread very quickly. There was nothing the doctors could do except make her comfortable. What about you?" Charlie said, looking up and surprising Frankie with the sudden change of focus. "You came here to escape something....or someone. Are you okay?"

This time, Frankie stopped walking as she weighed up what to say and how much to share. The village was silent, save the sound of the wind whistling through the trees, bare of leaves and creating sinister shadows on the ground in the moonlight.

"I came here to get away from my partner, Robert. We've been together for seven years, but it's not working," she paused, taking a deep breath of the chilled air. "I needed some time to think."

"Do you love him?" Charlie asked, trying to figure out why any man would let someone like Frankie go.

Frankie froze to the spot, rooted in uncertainty. Did she love Robert?

"I'm sorry, I shouldn't have asked that," said Charlie, rushing to ease Frankie's discomfort and chastising himself for being so thoughtless. "It's none of my business. I'm sorry."

"Don't be sorry. I'm not sure, is the answer. I used to love Robert. Now I'm not sure. That's why I'm here. I want to figure it all out without him around. Does that make sense?"

"It makes perfect sense to me. And if there is a single place in the world where you can clear your mind and connect with the majesty of nature, it is Bayscar."

As they walked down the track towards Elizabeth's cottage, they fell into an easy silence once more. An owl called from a nearby tree, and in the distance, they could hear the faint sound of the waves hitting the rocks far below the cliff carried inland on the breeze.

"This is where I leave you," said Charlie as they drew to a stop. Frankie looked at her cottage, grateful that she had left some lights on to welcome herself home. The track was poorly lit, and the cottage was in quite a lonely spot.

"Thank you for walking me home," she replied quietly, feeling unexpectedly shy in Charlie's company.

"Thank you for walking with me. I'll wait here until you're through the door. Have a good night."

"Thanks, Charlie. Maybe see you in the hotel tomorrow?" she asked as she walked down the short path past her car.

"I would think so. Not a huge amount else to do around here on a Friday night! Goodnight!"

As Frankie placed the key in the lock, Charlie turned and walked into the darkness, down the track to his own house, a half-mile away. The cottage was warm and welcoming, and having kicked off her shoes, Frankie set about making herself a hot chocolate and added a splash of cream liqueur to it as a treat.

Settling in front of the TV in her pyjamas, Frankie flipped through the channels, keeping her mind distracted from thinking about Charlie and Katie and all of the pain he had gone through. And, of course, his question. Did she still love Robert?

There was no straightforward answer, and that told Frankie everything she needed to know. She still cared about Robert. The real question was how much.

Chapter 9

To Frankie's relief, her job at the hotel was perfect for her new lifestyle. It provided enough flexibility to spend time walking and exploring the area, planning what she wanted to do to the cottage and spending time with Lilly, Tash and a few other women in the village. And Sue had offered her shifts at lunchtime and in the evenings, meaning her income was growing nicely, and so far, she could avoid the dreaded call to her parents requesting financial support.

Elizabeth had left a pot of money to cover the costs of refurbishing the cottage - or at least some of the costs - and Frankie was determined not to go near that for her personal use. So far, the hotel job was keeping her afloat, and it was a million times more enjoyable than talking to people on the phone. Ironically, it hadn't escaped Frankie's notice that the years of daily abuse and rudeness she had endured selling home improvements had created the perfect baseline for dealing with customers in a restaurant. The calm way Frankie could diffuse a difficult situation had become something of a gift for her colleagues, who happily deferred to Frankie when a tricky customer reared their head. Frankie didn't mind, and her confidence grew with each passing day.

It was now approaching April, and spring was in full bloom; the village full of daffodils, crocuses and every plant seemed to wake up and shoot. The weather was still chilly, but the sun was out most days, and the bay sparkled like an exquisite sea of diamonds when the sun was high in the sky, leaving Frankie exhilarated by the beauty of her surroundings.

As her self-confidence increased, Frankie started work on the cottage in earnest, painting the bathroom and spare bedroom without help. After some procrastination, she started sanding down the window frames inside, ready to gloss them as soon as it was warm enough to open the windows for any time without freezing half to death. Everything Frankie achieved gave her an immense sense of satisfaction. All the hours she had spent watching property renovation shows and dreaming of her own project one day were paying off at last. And it felt so good. So right.

There were limits to Frankie's abilities that she couldn't ignore, though, and the thorny issue of re-grouting the bathroom tiles was a constant concern. There was only one person Frankie knew well enough to ask for help, and that was Charlie. But she couldn't bring herself to mention it to him, her natural inclination towards shyness rearing its head each time Charlie was around. It was frustrating, and so despite Lilly's assurance that Charlie would love to help, Frankie's reluctance to ask remained in place, along with the mould and mildew in the bathroom.

Easter was just days away, and although the hotel was fully booked from Good Friday to Easter Monday, the restaurant was like a ghost town for Frankie's Tuesday evening shift. She was covering the shift alone, giving Byron some extra time to study for his A-Levels, and even then, Frankie was bored to sobs, looking out across the bay as darkness fell, with an empty restaurant reflecting in the window.

"Hey, you. Sue said you could call it a night if you want. She sent the chef's home early," said Lilly, strolling into the restaurant and joining Frankie to gaze across the bay.

"I'll never get tired of this view," said Frankie dreamily.

"Did you hear me? Sue said you could stop working. So why not come and have a drink with Charlie and me?"

Frankie tore her eyes from the window and smiled. "Sounds good. Let me just tidy table 3, and I'll meet you there."

Lilly left her to it as she cleared the dessert plates and glasses from the only table used all night. Within five minutes, she turned off the lights and walked to the front bar. The first thing she saw was Charlie, and he looked great in a denim shirt and jeans. Not many men could carry off double denim, but it seemed Charlie could. He looked a bit subdued as the conversation went on all around him, and then from nowhere, Lilly wrapped her arms around his shoulders and kissed him on the cheek. A whisper of jealousy washed through Frankie, and she quickly batted it away. She had no time for it. Life was complicated enough.

"Here she is!" called Sue, proffering a glass of wine over the bar towards Frankie, who accepted it gratefully.

"Thanks, Sue." Frankie opened her bag to dig out her purse.

"It's on the house, love. Put your money away."

"In that case, thank you again," said Frankie smiling broadly.

To Frankie's left, Lilly disentangled herself from Charlie and brushed his hair into place. Again, it was an intimate gesture, and again, Frankie felt something approaching jealousy. But if Lilly noticed, she didn't let on, and the conversation was soon flowing, with Pete joining the group after a few minutes.

"So, how're you getting on with the cottage, Frankie?

Made much progress?" asked Pete, nursing a pint with half an eye on reception, just in case.

"She's stuck. Aren't you Frankie?" said Lilly, much to Frankie's dismay.

"Stuck with what?" asked Charlie, as if on cue.

"Frankie has a few bits that need doing that she can't do herself. She needs someone to help her. Don't you, Frankie?"

"Lilly! Stop! It's fine. I can manage. I just need to watch a few YouTube videos, that's all. Nothing is so complicated I can't google it," Frankie laughed, hoping she had closed the issue down.

"I can help you," said Charlie, smiling directly at Frankie. "It would be good to have something to focus on at the moment."

Frankie looked at Lilly, who gave her a look Frankie didn't quite understand but recognised as a warning of some kind.

"Oh, Charlie, it's coming up to the anniversary again, isn't it?" said Sue sadly, earning her a dark look from Lilly.

"Three years," Charlie replied quietly. "I can't believe it's been three years already. So, I'd love to help you with whatever you need, okay? Look on it as you doing me a favour," he said, lifting his glass and tipping it at Frankie, who simply nodded in response.

"Okay, that's settled then," said Lilly, standing up. "Charlie, you can help Frankie get her bathroom sorted and anything else she needs help with and Frankie, you can entertain Charlie with your sparkling wit and distract him from how sad he will become over the next five days. Excellent. Well, I'm whacked. Staring at numbers all day is tiring work, so if you don't mind, I will head off."

"I'll come with you," said Frankie, draining her wine glass quickly. "I'll see you all tomorrow."

"I'll pop round after 11 if that's okay?" asked Charlie as Frankie stood up.

"Only if you're sure?" she asked, still uncomfortable with the idea despite Lilly's persistence.

"I'm very sure. See you tomorrow."

As Frankie and Lilly left the hotel, Lilly looped her arm through Frankie's, and they walked together as far as the end of the hotel driveway.

"Right. Goodnight, gorgeous woman. Have fun with Charlie tomorrow!" said Lilly, embracing Frankie.

"Honestly, Lilly, you are incorrigible! But thank you anyway. Have a good day tomorrow. Don't go too mad with your spreadsheets!"

"I'll try!" Lilly called as she turned and walked towards the parade of houses and small shops that formed the busiest part of the village.

Frankie watched her strut along the road, envious of her body confidence and presence. And as she turned to walk down the track and home to her little cottage, she fiercely batted away any suggestion that she was envious of anything else.

Charlie arrived at 11 as promised, and after three hours of scraping noises coming from the bathroom, he emerged looking dusty and, to Frankie's relief, happy. He was very gloomy when he arrived, saying little beyond hello, and then disappearing into the bathroom with a cup of tea. Frankie had popped her head round the door a couple of times with fresh cups of tea, but beyond that, he had gone about his task, leaving her to amuse herself with sanding the window frame in her bedroom.

"It's a bit of a mess in there, but I should be able to get it grouted before I go, and then it should be okay to use again by tomorrow night. Will that be okay?"

"Of course!" said Frankie, grateful that he was doing the work and in no way inclined to be inconvenienced by how long it would take. "Can I make you some lunch? I've got some ham and cheese and some fresh bread from Sam's bakery?"

"I will never say no to anything from Sam's! That man makes the best bread this side of Harrogate! Let me help you get it ready, though."

Charlie washed his hands in the kitchen sink, and then they both set about getting everything ready for lunch. Within ten minutes, all manner of deliciousness was laid out on the table. Sam's tiger bread smelled terrific, and Frankie had bought a variety of cheeses, some fresh ham from the butchers below Lilly's flat and even got some handmade crisps from Rose at the tearoom. It all looked great, and they sat down to eat next to the picture window overlooking the bay. A heavy mist had settled, and it looked like a storm was blowing in. Frankie never ceased to be amazed by the strength of the storms that blew in from the sea, and by the look of the clouds, another one was imminent.

"Have you heard from Robert?" Charlie asked between mouthfuls of bread and cheese.

"He texts me now and then, asks me when I'm coming home, but nothing more than that," Frankie replied. Robert sent her a message almost every week, usually on a Saturday, and it was always the same exchange. She knew his patience would break eventually, but things were repetitive, predictable, and thankfully unchallenging for now.

"And do you think you'll go home?"

The question was more direct than Frankie was expecting, and she took a moment to form a response, sipping her cup of coffee to buy herself some time.

"I don't know. I love it here. I love who I am here. But my home is down there, and I miss my parents…."

"And Robert?" Charlie asked, raising an eyebrow.

"I'm still not sure. It's complicated. He hurt me over and

over again, and he doesn't care. He humiliates me over and over again, and I am ashamed of myself for tolerating it, for allowing him to be so disrespectful of me…." Frankie was startled by how open she was and immediately changed the subject. "Anyway, how are you doing? You know, with everything?"

"Honestly, Frankie, I'm not sure either. In some ways, it gets a tiny bit easier every year, the pain of losing her, I mean. But I have so much guilt, and that never leaves me…."

"Guilt?" Frankie asked, unable to fathom what he could feel guilty about, based on the little she knew of him at least.

Charlie picked up his coffee and stared out the window as the dark clouds edged ever closer to land.

"I've never told anyone this before…" he began, before pausing again.

"Only say what you are comfortable to say, Charlie. I won't push you," Frankie said softly.

"I wasn't there enough. In the final days. I should have been there more…."

Frankie intuitively let the silence sit between them, her sense of empathy for how hard it was to share the most private thoughts far outweighing her curiosity.

At length, Charlie looked out towards the sea and began to speak quietly. "I was scared, and I couldn't face losing her. So, I worked. All the time. Constantly out in the fields, anywhere but in the house, with Katie." He began to cry, and Frankie reached for the box of tissues on the windowsill, placing it next to him without fanfare.

"Her parents begged me to come in, to be with her. I came in at the end. I was there when she died. But I should have been there more in her final days, Frankie. I let her down." He broke into sobs, and Frankie stood without thinking and walked around the table, sitting down next to him and holding him as he cried. Her need to comfort him was instinctive, and at that moment, she cared nothing for how little they knew each other. He needed to feel love and acceptance, and she could provide it.

They stayed together as he cried, expelling some of the built-up emotion and toxic guilt from his mind. And Frankie said nothing; no words would be enough. Outside, the storm had moved in, and without warning, the sky lit up with a flash of lightning as the rain began to hammer against the windows, water streaming down the hill outside, flowing back to the sea far below them. The circle of life, nature persisting outside the cottage despite the very human struggle taking place within.

"Thank you," said Charlie softly as he lifted his head at last.

Frankie pulled her arms away quickly, painfully aware of the fragility of the moment. She walked back to her side of the table, flicking the overhead light on as she moved past the switch.

"You did the best you could, Charlie. None of us knows how to cope when we face losing someone we love so much. But you were there at the end, and that's the most important thing, right? You were there when she needed to say goodbye."

"I was," he replied simply. "Thank you, Frankie. For listening, I mean. I've never told a soul any of that before; I was just too ashamed."

"There is nothing to be ashamed of, Charlie. We are all doing the best we can with what we have. Please be a bit gentler with yourself. You're a good man."

They held eye contact for a moment, and then Charlie smiled at her.

"You are a kind and caring woman, Frankie Gleane, and everything you have just said to me about not being ashamed and being gentler on myself, I am saying to you too. The way

Robert has treated you sounds appalling to me, from what little I know, and you have nothing to be ashamed about. We are both good people, Frankie. I needed to see that in myself today. And I hope you can see it in yourself too."

Frankie nodded, eyes brimming with tears.

Outside, the sun broke through the clouds, and they both watched as a rainbow appeared across the bay, and slowly, the rain began to stop falling.

Chapter 10

As the car pulled onto the driveway, Martin beeped his horn, and Frankie came running out of the cottage, buzzing with excitement. It had been almost three months since she had last seen her parents, and as Jane emerged from the car, Frankie wasted no time giving her an enormous hug.

"Oh, Mum, I have missed you so much!" she cried, pulling back and drinking in the sight of her mother.

"We've missed you too, darling. I can't believe it's been such a long time since you came up here. We should have come up sooner, but with one thing and another...."

"Frankie understands, Jane. Come here you!" Martin said, reaching for Frankie and cuddling her. "You look extremely well, young lady. A sight to behold."

"Wait till you see inside the cottage!" said Frankie, pulling away and walking towards the front door. The small garden in front of the cottage was in full bloom, with daffodils and tulips lining the edge of the lawn. Frankie had spent time weeding and making it look perfect, and she smiled with pride at how wonderful it looked as a result.

As they entered the cottage, the smell of a freshly baked cake was unmissable, and the sunshine yellow paint and carefully restored cupboard doors, which had taken Frankie a whole week to do, had given the entire space a new lease of life.

"The kitchen looks wonderful, Frankie. You've done a marvellous job on the cabinets. Very professional." Martin ran his finger along one of the doors and nodded his approval.

"Charlie helped. He showed me how to strip the old paint off. It was straightforward enough once I knew what to do," Frankie replied, playing down the hard physical labour it had required to achieve that smooth, freshly painted look.

Since their heart to heart at the end of March, Frankie hadn't seen much of Charlie. He locked himself away in his farmhouse for a few days to mark the anniversary of losing Katie, and then he'd been busy with lambing, so his visits to the hotel bar had all but stopped. The only person to see him recently was Lilly, who popped in to give him a hand on the weekend. Frankie had found herself missing him at the bar when she finished her shifts and was relieved to see him again two weeks ago after a hectic Friday night in the restaurant. They talked, and he offered to show her how to strip and repaint the kitchen cabinets, popping round the next day.

"Have you seen much of Charlie?" asked Martin, as if reading Frankie's mind.

"Not much lately. He's been busy with the lambs. Come into the living room, and you can see them in the field outside. They're so cute!"

Frankie pushed open the door and sure enough, just outside the window was a sheep and her three lambs following behind. And in the distance, the sun streamed through the clouds and down onto the bay. It was an idyllic scene, which Frankie was becoming increasingly attached to.

"Can I get you a cup of tea and some cake?" Frankie asked as both parents sat down.

"Yes, please!" said Martin quickly.

"Just you mind how much cake you give him, Frankie. His

last blood test wasn't great, and he's supposed to be watching how much sugar he eats - aren't you, Martin?" said Jane, pointedly.

"Just a small slice then, love," said Martin sheepishly.

Having served tea and cake, Frankie settled herself on the sofa opposite her parents. Seeing them with her here in her grandma's cottage was quite simply wonderful. They chatted for a while and caught up on the local gossip, and news about Jane's best friend Maureen, who had decided to dye her hair purple and quit her job to focus on her spirituality, much to the shock of her husband, Bill. Apparently, Aunty Jean had adopted another two cats, bringing her tally up to an impressive eleven and confirming her status in Frankie's mind, at least, as the mad cat lady. The one subject that didn't come up was Robert, and Frankie knew it was only a matter of time.

"I saw Robert the other day," said Martin, setting down his empty mug.

"Oh? Did you speak to him?" asked Frankie, wondering why Martin looked uncomfortable.

"No, dear. He was with someone. I just saw him in passing, really. He didn't see me...."

"Just tell her, Martin. She deserves to know," said Jane impatiently.

"Are you sure?" Martin asked, turning to Jane.

"Oh, for goodness' sake! He was with another woman, Frankie. At the garden centre on the ring road. They were holding hands." Jane sounded so matter-of-fact, Frankie almost broke into a smile, but she said nothing.

After a moment, Martin asked, "Have you heard from him at all, love?"

"He texts me about once a week. He tried to call me a couple of weeks ago, but I was on shift at the restaurant, and when I called him back, he didn't pick up. When he texts, it's the same thing all the time. He's sorry, he'll change if I will. He misses me, and he wants me back…."

"And how do you feel about that?" asked Jane.

"I don't feel anything much, Mum. Not about him. I'm numb, I guess. I know I need to face it and make a decision but every day seems like the wrong day to open myself up to it. So, I don't."

In reality, Robert was on Frankie's mind almost every day. Something would happen that would remind her of him, or she would recall a conversation or see something. Tiny little things that brought him to mind, and yet never enough to open herself up to the truth of what she felt. Never enough to make her face the emotions and hurt or make any decision about her future with him.

"Well, Ingrid, who lives four doors up from you and Robert, caught me in the supermarket last week and told me he's been bringing his fancy woman back to the house. It's not easy news to share, love, but you need to know what's going on." Watching Frankie closely, Jane plumped the cushion next to where she sat and placed it on her knee. "You seem so much happier up here, dear. The village seems to suit you. We'll support you if you decide to stay and not come back down south, won't we, Martin?"

"Yes! Of course, we will. We just want you to be happy, love. That's all we care about."

Frankie stood up and walked to the window, seeking distraction and solace in the beauty of the view across the fields to the sea and beyond. In the distance, she spotted Charlie, driving across one of his fields, with his two sheepdogs in the back of the truck. She watched as he wound his way carefully through the field, missing the roughest, rockiest areas and eventually, he disappeared behind the wall of trees that obscured his farmhouse from her view.

She turned to her parents and smiled. "I am happy here.

That's all I know at the moment. But it's enough."

It felt strange for Frankie to be sat in the restaurant, being served by Byron rather than taking orders herself. As she perused the menu, her parents chattered about the fantastic view the table offered and how they'd forgotten how magnificent the hotel's location was. For Frankie, there was less wonderment now. This was her place of work, and the view was hers to enjoy every day. The realisation made her smile to herself.

The family group managed to get through three delicious courses without any further mention of Robert or his 'fancy woman', and Frankie was able to relax and enjoy her parent's company. She heard all about Martin's plans for retirement and how Jane was considering joining a bridge club and wanted Martin to go with her. Martin's face told Frankie everything she needed to know about Martin's views on Bridge club, and it was evident to her at least that if Jane were going to the club, she would be going without her husband.

After dinner, they moved into the bar and took a table in the corner. Sue stepped out from behind the bar and brought their drinks over.

"It's so nice to meet you both at last! Frankie has told me all about you!" she said as she reached up to reposition the biro jammed into her incongruously high and messy bun. "And my condolences on the loss of Elizabeth, of course. We were all so saddened to hear of her passing."

"Thank you, Sue. We miss her dreadfully, don't we, Martin?" said Jane, sipping her Chardonnay.

"We certainly do. And we need to thank you, Sue. For employing our lovely daughter in your fine establishment. We are very grateful you gave her a chance."

Frankie was equal parts embarrassed and irritated by her dad's comment. He made it sound like Sue had done them a favour.

"Dad! I'm a pretty good waitress!" she said, laughing.

"It's true," said Sue. "She's a superstar waitress. We'd be lost without her, if I'm honest."

Someone coughed to get Sue's attention, and she sped back to serve them. It was a busy night in the bar, whereas the restaurant had been lovely and quiet.

A few minutes later, Lilly walked in, collected her usual drink from Sue and, spotting Frankie and her parents, made a beeline for their table and dropped down in the seat next to Frankie.

"You must be the parents! Great to meet you! I'm Lilly." She thrust her hand towards Martin for a vigorous shake before doing the same with Jane. "You have quite a fabulous daughter. We all love her. There's no way you can have her back down south. We are going to claim her for the North!"

Jane and Martin laughed, and Lilly winked at Frankie before taking a swig of her rum and coke. The foursome settled into light conversation, chatting about Frankie as a child, the cottage and Lilly even asked about Elizabeth, making Martin happy as he recounted stories about his mum. Frankie realised that Lilly managed to dodge most of the questions about herself. Although she chatted happily about her life in the village, she steered clear of talking about her life in Harrogate or her family. Thanks to Jane's careful persistence, Lilly shared that her father was Nigerian and her mother was Irish, which was news to Frankie, who had made several failed attempts to discover anything about Lilly's roots.

At around 10 pm, the group began to flag and were about to call it a night, when the bar door opened, and Charlie walked in.

"What time do you call this, young man?" said Pete playfully as he pulled a pint and handed it to Charlie over the bar.

"Another couple of lambs came tonight. I really need this drink!"

"Hey, you! Come and see Frankie's parents," called Lilly, grabbing a chair from another table and pulling up alongside her so Charlie could sit down.

Looking a little uncomfortable and extremely tired, Charlie walked over and smiled at Frankie before turning to shake Martin's hand. "Good to see you again, Martin."

"Charlie! Great to see you!' said Martin, standing to shake Charlie's hand and highlighting the difference in their heights. "This is my wife, Jane. I don't think you've met before."

Charlie reached across the table to shake Jane's hand, and for a moment, Frankie could swear her mum was blushing! "It's lovely to meet you, Charlie. We've heard a lot about you from Frankie."

It was Frankie's turn to blush, but Charlie came to her rescue.

"I'm sure there's not much to say about me! I've just shown you how to do a couple of things, haven't I, Frankie? And it's been good for me too. It's nice to have something a bit different to focus on."

"Well, we appreciate any help you've given, Charlie. It was a big deal, sending our girl up here to live on her own for a bit. Knowing you were around helped me and Jane sleep a bit easier in our beds. I can't tell you how hard it's been having her so far away," said Martin, raising his near-empty glass to Charlie.

"Well, he is our resident knight in shining armour, aren't you Charlie-boy?" said Lilly, ruffling his hair.

Jane raised an eyebrow, and Frankie felt the familiar and unwelcome sensation of jealousy rear its head again. There was a level of familiarity between Lilly and Charlie that

Frankie couldn't quantify, and the fact she felt she needed to was emotionally inconvenient, to say the least.

Charlie entertained the group with stories of his lambing, and without anyone asking, Pete delivered another round of drinks and melted away into the background. Frankie had no idea how the hotel made any kind of profit, but she loved Sue and Pete and how welcome they had made her - and her family - feel.

"Right, well, I think we should head off to bed, Jane dear. We need to be ready for the journey up to Durham to see Bob and Carol in the morning, and it's still a fair distance, even from here," said Martin, stifling a yawn. "Frankie, dear. Will you walk us to our room?"

"Yeah, of course." She turned to Lilly and Charlie. "I'll see you both tomorrow, maybe?"

Lilly nodded, then rested her head on Charlie's shoulder. "I can wait and walk you home if you like?" Charlie said to Frankie. "It's on my way."

"Are you sure? That would be wonderful, Charlie. It's a dark track, and I do worry…." began Martin before Jane pulled him away and towards the stairs.

Frankie rolled her eyes, embarrassed at how protective her dad was being, and she tried desperately not to blush. "Only if you want to, Charlie. I'm sure I'll be fine if you want to get home…."

"He'll wait," said Lilly sleepily, and Charlie nodded.

Martin opened the door, and they walked into the bedroom. It was one of the hotel's nicest rooms, with uninterrupted views across the bay through the large picture window, next to the king-sized canopy bed.

"That Charlie's a good-looking man, isn't he?" said Jane, linking arms with Frankie and pulling her to sit on the bed.

"I hadn't noticed," Frankie lied. She plainly had noticed. It was hard to miss. Men who looked as good as Charlie were few and far between.

"I think he and Lilly make a lovely couple, don't you, Martin?" Jane called across the cavernous room as Martin took off his jacket and hung it on the back of a decorative chair.

"They do indeed."

"Have they been together long, love?" Jane asked as she eased off her shoes, paying no attention to the look of intense discomfort on her daughter's face.

It had never occurred to Frankie that Charlie and Lilly were together. Like, properly together. But now Jane had mentioned it; it made sense. Sue had said that Charlie had been miserable for ages and only started to smile again a few months ago. Maybe that was when he got together with Lilly? They were so close. But then she remembered he was still wearing his wedding ring, and the idea of them being together collapsed as quickly as it had sprung up just moments before.

"I don't think they're together, Mum. He still wears his wedding ring. His wife died three years ago."

"Well, it won't be long, you mark my words. That girl has her sights set on him, and I don't see him putting up any kind of a struggle. Give it a few more weeks, and you'll be the third wheel, my dear! Just wait and see! I'm rarely wrong in matters of the heart, am I Martin?"

"No, dear," Martin shouted from the bathroom.

"Right, I'm going to head off. Charlie's waiting for me in the bar," Frankie stood up.

"With Lilly," said Jane, hammering home her theory to an unimpressed audience of one.

"Night, Mum, love you. Night, Dad! I'll see you both at the cottage for breakfast at 9 am, okay?"

"We'll be there, sweetheart. Love you!" said Jane, as

Frankie closed the door and rested herself against it.

Charlie and Lilly. Why hadn't she realised?

In the bar, Charlie was chatting to Pete and Lilly, and faced with the sight of them all together talking comfortably as a group, Frankie felt an overwhelming desire to be on her own.

"You all set?" Charlie asked, seeing her walk in.

"Are you okay, lovely?" asked Lilly. "You look like you've seen a ghost! Look at her, Charlie. She's white as a sheet!"

"Come on, let's get you home," said Charlie, and the three of them waved goodnight to Pete and stepped out into the cool night air.

Lilly chatted away with Charlie until they got to the end of the hotel driveway, with Frankie a few steps behind. Lilly gave her a hug goodnight and then hugged Charlie before walking the short distance up the hill to her flat. Charlie watched her walk away, and Frankie watched him.

Eventually, once it was clear Lilly had made it to her front door, Charlie turned, and the two of them walked in silence down the track.

"Are you okay? Did something happen? Have you heard from Robert?" he asked, eyes shining with unconcealed concern.

"I'm fine. Just tired. It's been a long day." Frankie knew she was lying; she felt more awake than ever, her mind racing over everything she might have missed, all the signs she should have spotted and inevitably, what it meant for her. And for Robert.

"Well, try and get a good night's sleep, and I'll maybe see you tomorrow, okay?" Charlie said as they stopped at the cottage.

"I will. Thanks, Charlie," said Frankie, believing that a decent night's sleep was as likely as winning the lottery.

She closed her front door and kicked off her shoes,

determined to pull herself together. By the time she opened the bedroom door, she felt a bit less tense, and once her make-up was washed off and she was safely wrapped in the warmth of her favourite fleece pyjamas, she knew everything would be okay. She didn't care about Charlie; of course, she didn't. She was just hurt and humiliated by Robert, and Charlie was the first man to show her any kindness in years. It was as simple as that. Charlie was nothing more than a distraction - albeit a very good looking one. If he wanted to be with Lilly, then it was fine.

As he walked down the dark track towards the old farmhouse, Charlie tried to make sense of his feelings. The third anniversary of losing Katie felt like it should be a turning point, somehow, like he should start to live again. Katie would want that; she had said as much in one of their last conversations before she slipped into her final sleep. The moon appeared from behind a cloud and slightly illuminated the ground at his feet. Taking advantage of the unexpected light, Charlie pulled his left hand from the warmth of his pocket and held it in front of him, his wedding ring glinting in the gentle moonlight.

"What do you think, Katie? I still miss you so much. I'm not sure I'm ready," he said quietly, looking up at the clouds moving across the endless dark of the night.

The silence that followed was not unexpected, and yet, in the face of all logic, Charlie still felt the familiar grief and disappointment that he could no longer seek counsel from his beloved wife. She would know what to do; he was sure of that. Katie always knew what was best for him, even when Charlie couldn't see it. The memory of her wisdom made him smile softly, and as he approached the farm gates, Katie's beloved dog, Sasha, came running to meet him, followed by her brother Zeus.

The loneliness of the farmhouse enveloped him completely as he walked through the door and turned on the lights. The dogs were running around excitedly, yet Charlie ached for something more. But looking at the ring again, this time in the stark bright light of the kitchen, he knew it wasn't time to take it off just yet. The time would come, but for now, it needed to stay exactly where Katie had placed it on their wedding day.

Chapter 11

The revolving door to the kitchen was in constant motion as Frankie, Bryon, Sue, and a somewhat reluctant Lilly moved to and fro, delivering the first course to all 100 wedding guests. Pete was moving from table to table, pouring wine for everyone, and in the background, carefully selected ambient music was barely audible against the buzz of chatter and excitement.

It wasn't often that the Bayscar Hotel hosted a wedding, and on the rare occasion that it happened, every available pair of hands was put to good use. To prove the point, Charlie had been summoned to man the bar while Pete served the guests at their tables. The hotel was nothing if not a community labour of love.

With the guests happily tucking into their prawn cocktail or soup starters, Frankie and Lilly took a moment to rest at the side of the room, gathering their strength before clearing the plates and moving on to deliver the main course.

"I don't know why I always agree to do this," said Lilly, taking a swig of her bottle of water. "Every time I say I'm never doing it again, Sue comes at me with those big eyes, and I'm powerless to turn her down. So why do I never learn?"

"Because it's such a worthwhile thing to do! Look at how

happy everyone is? Weddings are special occasions. And it means the world to Sue and Pete. You know it does...."

"Yep, and they've been good to me too. But even so, all this wedded bliss and forced joy make me feel a bit queasy."

"What? What are you on about? It's lovely! When did you get so jaded and cynical about weddings?" Frankie asked, incredulous that her open-minded and optimistic friend had such a dim view of marriage.

"Let's just say, big white weddings aren't my thing. Just one of the many reasons I left Harrogate...." Lilly replied before walking away and leaving Frankie confused and deeply intrigued.

Even after three months of friendship, Lilly was still very mysterious about her life in Harrogate. Frankie knew very little about her life before she came to Bayscar, and even Charlie wouldn't be drawn when she asked him about Lilly a couple of weeks ago. So, Frankie's best guess was a relationship gone wrong, and Lilly's antithesis to big weddings definitely didn't contradict the theory. But there was obviously more to it. Frankie just wasn't sure she would ever find out what.

But for now, it didn't matter. The conversation level had risen, which was a sure sign most people had finished eating, and it was safe to clear the tables for the main course. The team sprang into action, and the tables were systematically cleared with a clatter of plates and cutlery. The kitchen was filled with piles of plates, bowls and silverware, ready for Byron's younger sister Ebony to wash up. Ebony herself was barely visible behind the stack of dirty dishes, but she seemed happy enough with her earbuds in and humming along to her music.

When the meal was over, it was time for the speeches, leaving Frankie, Lilly, Byron and Sue with a solid 20-minute break before serving the coffee. They collapsed into a booth in the bar, and Pete brought over some drinks for them all. Frankie looked around for Charlie, but he was nowhere to be seen. She was about to ask where he was when Lilly beat her to it.

"I take it Charlie's gone home for a bit?" she asked Pete as he sat down next to Sue.

"Yeah. One of the dogs was unwell, and he wanted to check on her. He said he'll be back in a bit before the bar gets busy again."

Lilly pulled her mobile from her pocket and started sending a message, which Frankie assumed was to Charlie. Since her parent's visit in early April, the idea of Charlie and Lilly being a couple had become something Frankie had learned to accept as inevitable. They were so close, and in many ways, Frankie was happy that they had found happiness with each other. But the possibility of them being together also forced her to think about her relationship with Robert. He had started calling her on a Saturday morning, and they were getting on okay again. However, he was still insistent that she should come home, and Frankie was resolute in her desire to stay in Bayscar for the time being. But both Robert and Frankie knew that with May just days away, the months were ticking by, and the chances of their relationship surviving were becoming increasingly slim.

The Groom's speech came to a conclusion, and the guest broke out in cheers and applause, signalling the need for the hotel team to swing into action once more and deliver the coffee and tea. With as much energy as they could muster, Frankie and Lilly moved from table to table, pouring hot drinks in the cups held aloft by guests who were, in many cases, totally unable to hold said cups very steadily at all. It was precarious work, and by the time all drinks had been safely delivered, Frankie and Lilly were both shattered.

"You two go and have another sit down in the bar. I'll call you when they all start to move into the other room. Then we can clear away the tables, set up for the buffet, and you are both done for the day," said Sue gratefully. She knew she relied on a considerable amount of goodwill to keep her hotel running, and she never missed an opportunity to show her gratitude. "I'll get Lee to bring out some sandwiches for you both…and some fries too."

Lilly teased her shoes off and rubbed her feet, and Frankie sat back against the cushioned seat and closed her eyes. Working at the hotel was exhilarating and exhausting all at once.

"Ah, there he is. Come and sit with us, Charlie!" called Lilly, and as if responding to a command, Charlie dutifully walked over and sat down.

"How's Sasha?" Lilly asked.

"I think she'll be okay. She's just a bit off colour. She probably ate something in the field. She seems a bit brighter now than earlier, so I'm less worried. How are you two? Glad that's all over a done with?"

"It's not over yet," said Frankie. "We still have to clear everything away and set up for the buffet." As she spoke, she pulled a face and Charlie, sat directly opposite her, found himself noticing how cute she looked when her nose wrinkled up that way, and he shifted his attention to his drink before anyone could see.

But Lilly saw the look on his face as he watched Frankie, and she smiled to herself as he made a considerable effort to look as disinterested as possible.

"You okay, Charlie?" she asked playfully, earning a hard stare from Charlie in response. "I think I'll go and see what Lee's doing with those sandwiches. I'm starving."

Left on their own, Frankie and Charlie fell into an

awkward silence, as was often the case these last few weeks. He had no idea what had happened on the evening of her parent's visit, but there had been an unmistakable distance between him and Frankie since that night. A distance he just couldn't understand.

"Lilly said she hates weddings," said Frankie, absentmindedly, her finger tracing the rim of her glass, her eyes cast down. "She's a very mysterious woman."

"She has some family stuff she's trying to figure out, that's all. She's not as cynical as she makes out. She's just trying to protect herself." Charlie couldn't say any more than that and probably should have said far less. But he was becoming more and more uncomfortable with how little Frankie knew about Lilly despite their growing friendship. Sooner or later, Lilly would need to be much more open - if she was ever going to settle in the village.

"I hope she's okay. Lilly deserves to be happy. She is such a wonderful person," Frankie replied, watching Charlie closely, frustrated by the dynamic that seemed to exist between the three of them. It was apparent to Frankie that as the newest member of the friendship group, she should rightfully sit on the periphery for a while, but they were drawing her in and holding her back at the same time. Her friendship with Charlie and Lilly had become important - a lifeline almost - at a time in her life when she needed people around that she could trust, and she trusted them both implicitly. But it was clear to her that they didn't trust her in the same way yet. Perhaps they would in time, but with no idea how long she would stay in Bayscar, Frankie was scared that time might run out.

Sunday morning dawned, and Frankie slept through the church bells, climbing from her bed long after the congregation had gone home and just in time to see the

Nordic Walking Club members stride past the cottage for their regular elevenses at the teashop. Shocked at how long she'd slept, Frankie leapt from the bed, searching for caffeine and something to eat.

As she watched the ships move across the bay, eating her toast and locally made plum jam, her phone lit up with an incoming call. It was Robert, and her heart sunk like a stone in her chest.

"Hello?"

"Frank, it's me. Can you talk?" Robert sounded like he was in a no-nonsense mood, and Frankie braced herself for what he had called to say.

"I have a few minutes," she lied. The entire day, or at least the entire afternoon, was clear, and she had no plans to do anything beyond watching old movies and going for a walk.

"I think we need to move this situation forward. One way or the other."

"And how do we do that?" Frankie asked, provocatively and fully recognising how annoyed Robert would become if she carried on.

"You need to come home so we can talk everything through face to face. All this texting and an occasional phone call isn't making any difference, is it? And I'm not prepared to wait around forever."

"I'm not asking you to, Robert." And she wasn't.

There was silence at the end of the phone, and Frankie took a sip of her coffee, trying to picture Robert in her mind's eye. But all she could see was him standing with his glass of whiskey and laughing at her that fateful last night before she left to come up to Yorkshire. The memory made her feel uncomfortable.

"I want us to give it another try, Frankie, and I am not willing to debate the matter over the phone. So, if you don't come to me, I'll come to you."

Frankie's heart sank. The idea of Robert coming to Bayscar felt like an invasion. This was her perfect world, her safe place, untainted by Robert or how he made her feel.

"I don't want you to come up, Robert. You don't know where I am anyway?" Frankie replied, a hint of defiance in her voice, despite the adrenalin coursing through her veins.

"It won't be hard to find you, Frankie. Trust me. I have a good idea where you are. I know your gran used to live up there. Someone told me at the funeral. So, I'll come up in the next couple of weeks," Robert said, his voice ringing with how pleased with himself he felt.

Frankie couldn't bear how smug he was being. And worse still, the fact that he was right and he could find her. "I don't want you to come," she said simply.

"I didn't want you to go. And sometimes, Frankie, we have to accept we can't have what we want. I'll be in touch." And with that, he hung up.

Frankie put her phone on the table, her hands shaking violently and her heart racing. This was her worst nightmare. Robert in Bayscar. She couldn't breathe and pushed open the window for some fresh air.

Unable to calm herself, the thought of Robert visiting was overwhelming, and so Frankie turned to Lilly for help. An emergency phone call and thirty minutes later, Frankie was secure in Lilly's sporty old hatchback, being whisked out of the village to Lilly's favourite coastal town and a tasty pub lunch.

"What you need, my lovely friend is to feel the sand between your toes, and I have got just the spot. Let's grab some lunch, and then I'll take you to my secret beach."

"Thanks, Lilly. I really appreciate this. I feel so wound up at the thought of him coming up here," said Frankie as she watched the trees fly past. Lilly wasn't a big believer in speed limits, it seemed.

In record time, they arrived in the quaint village of Pictborough, located just across the bay from Bayscar and a lovely pub right on the harbour, which afforded them views back across the bay and a clear view of the Bayscar hotel, albeit very far in the distance, perched high on its headland.

"This place is gorgeous, Lilly! How did you find it?" asked Frankie, taking in the overall ambience and feeling immediately at home.

"I came here a lot with my ex a couple of years ago," Lilly replied without taking her eyes from the menu.

"Does he live nearby then?"

"What? Oh, no. We just liked it here." Lilly seemed flustered by Frankie's question and appeared to shut down. And once again, Frankie felt like Lilly was holding back. It made her sad that even now, in the face of her problems with Robert, which she had freely shared in recent weeks, Lilly still felt she had to be careful around Frankie.

"Are you okay, Lilly? You seem a bit tense."

Lilly looked up from the menu, and it was clear that Frankie was genuinely concerned about her. She knew it was probably time to be honest with Frankie, but no matter how hard she tried, the words wouldn't come. So few people knew the truth, and after everything that happened in Harrogate, no matter how wrong it was to be so secretive, life was undeniably simpler when people drew their own assumptions. But she would tell Frankie soon. Definitely.

"I'm okay. Just tired after last night. That wedding reception went on and on!" It was a blatant attempt to change the subject, but Frankie chose to run with it, to Lilly's relief.

"You didn't need to stay till the end, though! We could have gone home after the buffet was put out, but I saw that bridesmaid dragging you onto the floor when that ABBA song came on! It's your own fault you're so tired!"

"You can talk! I didn't see you rushing home for a hot chocolate either! It was a good laugh, though, wasn't it? They were a good crowd."

"They were…." Frankie was interrupted by the arrival of someone to take their order and the complex decision she now had to make on the hoof.

After the delicious lunch, they ambled back to the car in a sleepy food haze. The drive to the beach was far more sedate than the drive to the pub two hours earlier, and Frankie enjoyed being able to take in some of the scenery that surrounded her life in Bayscar. Somewhere between Pictborough and Bayscar, Lilly turned down a narrow single-track road with no signpost.

"Where are we going?" asked Frankie, bewildered by the apparent invisibility of their intended destination.

"Just wait and see," said Lilly as they drove slowly through small clusters of houses dotted along the track - too small to call villages.

After about ten minutes, the track came to its natural end with no sign of any coastline ahead. Frankie was perplexed as Lilly pulled the car into a makeshift car park at the side of the road. "Shall we get out?" she asked, smiling.

"Okay…." Frankie replied, hoping there wasn't a long hike ahead and looking down at her shoes, judging them wholly unsuited to any kind of rough terrain.

A footpath began where the road stopped, and although overgrown and canopied by trees, it wasn't muddy or rough, and Frankie's shoes looked to be suitable for the time being. A quick look at Lilly's Birkenstocks reassured her that no rocky terrain was imminent, and she relaxed a little. The path continued for a few hundred yards, and there was no indication of anything coastal beyond the call of seagulls in the distance. But Frankie kept faith with her friend. Lilly had never let her down yet.

And sure enough, as the path turned to the left, the trees began to clear, and Frankie began to hear the sea in the distance, the gentle sound of waves lapping the shore. The path led down a steep decline, and a tiny beach was at the bottom. No signs, no people. Just a tiny patch of sand in an inlet with a little building tucked up on a platform and accessible by a wooden walkway.

"This is amazing!" cried Frankie as she rushed forward to the sand.

"You need to get those shoes off! I want your feet in that water pronto! Sand between your toes, right? That was the deal!" said Lilly, beaming at the joy on Frankie's face as she kicked off her shoes and ran onto the sand. The reality of adulthood would come crashing back down upon her shoulders soon enough. But for the time being, Frankie looked like a child, lost in a world of innocence.

She ran into the sea, squealing at how cold the water was as it washed up to her ankles. But she stayed put, walking backwards and forwards along the tiny beach, wiggling her toes in the sand and drinking in the sensation of freedom and magic that comes from being so close to the sea after so many weeks of watching it from high on a cliff.

Stood alone on the shoreline, lost in her own thoughts, Lilly's heart sang with the joy of seeing her friend experience such presence, happiness and freedom - even if only for a moment - a moment that Lilly herself longed for but feared would never come, despite all of Charlie's assurances and support.

Chapter 12

Frankie paced around the living room, moving things around pointlessly, her whole body humming with nervous energy. She felt sick to her stomach and exhausted after a long sleepless night, tossing and turning and working through endless imaginary conversations with the man who was about to arrive any minute.

Robert had called on Tuesday to tell Frankie he would be arriving on Thursday afternoon. There was no hint of any flexibility. He was coming whether she liked it or not, so her shift at the hotel was swapped with Byron, and her plans to work with Charlie on ripping out and replacing the decking outside the bedroom were placed on hold. Charlie had offered to be there when Robert arrived, in case Frankie needed any support, and although grateful, Frankie turned the offer down. She had to face Robert alone, whether she wanted to or not.

Having said he would arrive around 2 pm, Frankie was surprised when he called at 2.15 to say he was stuck in traffic and would be around an hour late. It was music to her ears but only provided a temporary reprieve, and now, it was approaching 3.30, and Robert's car was pulling into the village and winding its way down the track to the cottage. Frankie's hands were ice cold, and she steeled herself for what lay ahead. No amount of imaginary conversation could foretell how this catch up would play out.

Three sharp knocks on the door announced his arrival, and Frankie opened the door and came face to face with Robert for the first time in close to four months. Without a word from either of them, Frankie stepped aside, and he walked in, taking in every detail of the homely kitchen and flowers on the windowsill. Then, without being invited to, he pushed open the door to the living room and walked in, dropping it behind him and allowing it to fall against Frankie's shoulder. It was a gesture of defiance and ignorance, and if he had intended to intimidate Frankie, it hadn't worked. As the door fell on her, all Frankie could feel was anger.

"Nice place," Robert said as he looked out of the window at the sea far below the cliff. "Nice view too. Not sure about all the sheep being so close, though. Bet they smell."

Frankie ignored his remark. "Do you want a drink?"

"A coffee would be nice, thanks for asking."

Without another word, Frankie went back out to the kitchen, and with hands shaking so hard she could barely pick up a spoon, she managed somehow to make Robert a coffee and carry it back into the living room without spilling a drop.

"Not having one?" he asked, placing the mug on the table next to where he sat.

"No."

"Are you going to be this standoffish for my whole visit, Frank? I didn't drive all this way for you to be non-communicative and ignorant."

"Why are you here, Robert?" she asked, sitting down opposite him and maintaining eye contact, determined not to be manipulated or intimidated.

"You know why I'm here. To sort out our relationship and make you see sense."

"Make me see sense? That's a joke. It's you who needs to see sense; it's you who thinks it's ok to jump from one affair to another without thinking of the consequences."

Robert said nothing, instead taking off his jacket and laying it next to him, smoothing out any creases.

"Robert, there's no point in you being here if you refuse to see any fault in yourself. I don't want to argue with you. I'm past all of that. I just want you to understand what you've done and how much you've hurt me," Frankie explained, her hands clasped so tightly together on her lap that her knuckles were white.

"I know I mistreated you, Frank. I can see that. Honestly, I can. But it wasn't just me, was it? You weren't exactly the most exciting girlfriend…." He trailed off, sensibly judging that saying anything more would inflame the situation beyond the point of no return.

"Define an exciting girlfriend, Robert? What was I supposed to do? Belly dance naked around the kitchen every night when you got home? For goodness' sake!" Frankie held her head in her hands, unable to look at him and not become overwhelmed with anger. Seeing him again had raised so much anger within her; it was incredible. Her urge to punch something - ideally Robert - was all-consuming.

"Maybe we should go for a walk?" Robert suggested, out of nowhere. "You could show me around, take me to that bench you talk about all the damn time and seem to love so much…."

Frankie sat for a moment and weighed up her options. Stay in here with Robert and argue endlessly until he finally went home, or go out into the sunshine and fresh air, still argue, but at least have something nice to look at while she was doing it.

"Okay. I'll get my jacket."

They walked up towards the hotel and took a route that tracked around the outer edge of the golf course, ostensibly to ensure as far as possible that Robert and Charlie didn't cross paths. Of course, it meant an increased risk of bumping into other people from the village, but somehow that didn't feel as terrible as Robert and Charlie coming face to face.

The conversation was light, much to Frankie's surprise. Robert asked questions about the village, where she had travelled in the area. They talked about her trip with Lilly to Pictborough and the tiny inlet with the beach, and Robert laughed when Frankie relayed her experience of paddling in the icy cold sea and squealing like a child. They sat on Frankie's favourite bench, and Robert listened carefully for the sound of the waves hitting the rocks far below. He told Frankie about a promotion he'd been offered and updated her on the gossip from around town, and Frankie couldn't shake the impression they were simply two friends, catching up after a long absence.

As if understanding the importance of making a good impression, the bay was magnificent, reflecting the blue sky above and yet still somehow changing colour as the clouds travelled across and obscured the sun every now and then. Gulls flew overhead, and the breeze was gentle and refreshing, the grasses surrounding the bench and the edge of the cliff moving to and fro, like a thousand tiny dancers all moving to the same piece of music. As the sun moved lower in the sky, the conversation shifted slightly to the funeral and the events that followed, and yet, as if hypnotised by the beauty of their environment, tempers didn't fray. They talked calmly and without accusation and blame, and it felt okay. Perhaps it was the scenery, maybe it was genuine emotion, but for the first time in a long time, Frankie saw the slightest flicker of possibility between them.

They stayed on the bench until it became too cold, the sun

now hidden by a blanket of cloud and the sea a heavy grey, withdrawing out with the tide and leaving the shiny rocks and slimy seaweed in its wake. They strolled back to the cottage along the same route they had taken earlier. As they passed the teashop, Rose stepped out to move the tables and chairs inside so she could close for the night, stopping to stare at Frankie and the mysterious man in her company.

"Hi, Rose!" Frankie called across the street, deciding it was better to face the issue head-on than be the subject of village gossip tomorrow. "This is, Robert. My, um, partner. He's come up to see me from home." It sounded awkward, but it was true.

"Hello, dear!" Rose called back. "Nice to meet you. Quite the girl you've got there. We all adore young Frankie!"

Frankie blushed, and Robert smiled, piling on the charm as only he could. "She is something special. I'll give you that. Lovely to meet you too, Rose."

Rose waved and then returned to the task at hand, leaving Frankie and Robert to continue their walk, turning right and following the track back down to the cottage. The peace and quiet of the walk were interrupted by an engine approaching behind them, and they stepped aside to allow the vehicle to pass. But Frankie's heart sank when she saw it was Charlie, and she hoped more than anything that he would keep on driving and stay in his truck.

He seemed inclined to do just that and simply waved as he drove past the pair. But it soon became clear there was an issue, and his truck drew to a standstill just outside Frankie's cottage. He climbed out, and Frankie's heart began to race. What was this about?

"Is that your car?" Charlie asked Robert without introduction.

"What if it is," Robert replied, and Frankie cringed at his bolshy attitude. This was not going to go well.

"It's blocking the track, and I can't get the truck through," said Charlie.

Frankie could tell he was uncomfortable. She hadn't ever seen him look so tense, and alarm bells rang in her mind as Robert stepped forward and past Charlie to look at the problem for himself.

"You could get a bus through that gap! Can't you drive, man?"

"What did you say to me?" Charlie walked towards Robert, who, faced with the fact that Charlie towered over him, instinctively stepped back.

"Please don't do this!" pleaded Frankie, as the men squared up against each other. "If either of you thinks anything of me, don't do this! Robert, move your car. Please!"

Both men looked at Frankie, and she thought it would be okay for a second. But then something seemed to shift in Robert, and he stepped away and began pacing in an agitated state. Charlie looked at Frankie, and she shrugged, and this small act was all it took to trigger Robert's outburst.

"Oh my God! This is him, isn't it? This is the guy who's been helping you with the cottage!" Robert shouted, still pacing. "It's Charlie, isn't it?" he asked, turning to face Charlie directly, but he didn't wait for an answer.

"So let me get this straight…. I'm down south, living in the house we used to share, the home we created, sleeping in the bed that we shared, while you are up here with him! And you seriously expect me to believe that you two are just friends?"

Frankie's mouth fell open in horror as Robert continued his tirade of abuse and accusations, shouting them loud for all to hear. What had happened to the calm, friendly man who had chatted amiably on the bench just minutes ago? Robert's mood changed in the blink of an eye, consumed by jealousy of his supposed love-rival, and he began to swear, insulting both Charlie and Frankie in equal measure. He worked himself into such a frenzy that it seemed unbelievable that one man could create such a scene. The fragile spell, bound by their time chatting on the cliff, was broken, shattered into fragments. Robert would never change.

At the top of the hill, Rose stepped out of her teashop and locked the door, humming to herself, when she heard someone shouting. It took no time for her to see that there was a situation building just outside Elizabeth's cottage down the hill. Without missing a beat, she pulled her phone from her bag and made two phone calls. One to Pete at the hotel, and the other to Lilly. Both were summoned, and both told Rose not to worry and to head off home, and they would come down and support Frankie.

The calmness with which Pete and Lilly had spoken to Rose dissipated quickly as they both ran down the track, and it was apparent Pete was a little out of condition as they reached the fray that was being played out. Robert was in a fury, seemingly fuelled by Charlie's complete lack of engagement. Charlie simply stood and listened as the list of Robert's accusations accumulated - sleeping with his girlfriend, poisoning Frankie against him and last but certainly not least, being a terrible driver.

Lilly raced to Frankie's side and checked she was okay. All Frankie could do was nod grimly, eyes fixed on Robert as he paced up and down, his face becoming more and more red. Lilly looped her arm over Frankie's shoulder and pulled her close, then moved her towards the cottage and out of range should the situation deteriorate into a physical fight.

Pete walked over to Charlie. "You okay, mate?"

"Well, I've been better. This guy is mental! Look at him!"

Robert was now standing next to his car and Charlie's truck, laughing at the 'acres of space' between them and shouting that he thought Charlie's taste in cars was obviously just like his taste in women - boxy and practical.

And for Charlie - this last taunt was the final straw. It was enough; Robert had crossed a line. To insult Frankie was unacceptable, but he was also insulting his beloved wife, Katie, which was simply unforgivable. Pete knew from the flicker in Charlie's eye what was going to happen next but stood by helpless. Charlie strode over to Robert, pulled his arm back and punched him square on the jaw. Robert crumpled to the floor instantly, clutching his face like the pathetic child his behaviour showed him to be.

In case Robert fought back, Pete raced over, but he needn't have worried. There was no fight left in Robert whatsoever, and Charlie walked away and over to Frankie and Lilly.

"I'm sorry you both had to see that," he said quietly, rubbing the knuckles on his right hand. "I'm not usually a violent man, but I will not stand by and allow someone like him to be so disrespectful." He turned to look at Frankie. "Not to you or anyone else."

"I'm so sorry, Charlie. I don't know what to say. He's not normally like that." Frankie didn't understand why she was trying to explain or support Robert's behaviour. The whole experience mortified her.

Robert quietly stepped into his car without fanfare or further objection and started the engine. But instead of moving it a few feet forward to let Charlie pass, he swung it hard around and sped up the track and away from the group. For some reason, Frankie found this funny, amused by the fact he had stormed off like a spoiled child. As she giggled, Lilly joined in, and within seconds the two women were doubled over in laughter; all of the nerves and tension of the row coming out in laughter so intense both women had tears streaming down their faces.

When things had calmed down, and both Frankie and Lilly had finally stopped laughing - and it took a few minutes - Pete walked Lilly home, leaving Frankie and Charlie alone.

"Are you going to be okay?" he asked, touching the top of Frankie's arm tenderly.

"I think so. He seems to have blown himself out. If he comes back, I'll tell him there's nothing between us, and I'm pretty sure he knows that anyway. He should know me better than to think I would be in a relationship with someone else while I have so much unfinished business with him. And I'm sorry, Charlie. I'm sorry he has been so awful to you and so rude. And those things he said - you know he was talking about me, right? He doesn't even know about Katie. He could never have said anything that was about her. It was all about me…."

Charlie watched as Frankie's eyes filled with tears, her need for him to understand the insults were for her, and that somehow that made it okay, tore at his heart and burned his soul.

"Even if he was talking about you, Frankie, it doesn't make it okay. You are worth so much more than that man. Honestly, you deserve to be cherished…." He paused, conscious that he had probably said too much. "Try and have a good evening, okay? And if you need me for anything, call me. I can be here in minutes. Promise me?"

"I promise," Frankie said quietly, but her mind was racing, rolling the word 'cherished' around and trying to remember why it felt so familiar, without success. "Good night, Charlie. Thank you for understanding."

Charlie walked to his truck without another word, started the engine, and drove down the track. Frankie watched him go, not moving, even when all that was left was an empty track in the failing light. A storm was blowing in.

As she walked towards the cottage, the word 'cherished' ran through her mind again, and she knew exactly what she needed to do to figure it out.

Once inside, she revelled in the silence, and having taken

off her shoes, went to her bedroom and opened the drawer next to the bed, retrieving the letter from her grandma.

She scanned the writing, trying to find what she was looking for quickly in case Robert came back. And then she saw it:

' ...he doesn't cherish you. And you should be cherished, my darling girl'

Darkness fell, and a storm blew in. Thunder clapped above the cottage, and the sky lit up as lightning snapped across the bay. It was the most spectacular light show on earth. Three short raps on the door announced Robert's return, and without a word, he walked through the door as Frankie held it open and sheepishly sat down in the lounge.

Frankie raided the freezer for a bag of frozen peas and handed them to Robert to hold against his face and take down some of the swelling. He sat with a look of intense shame and self-loathing. This was not the scenario he'd imagined on his long drive up to Yorkshire, and a part of him wished he hadn't bothered.

Taking pity on his pathetic state, Frankie ordered a pizza. She gave him options, but Robert said he didn't care what he ate, and he soon regretted this when it became clear that chewing pizza dough with a bruised jaw was a sight harder than consuming noodles or rice. Whilst he struggled to marry the pain in his face with his need for food, Frankie could do nothing more than watch with the slightest hint of amusement. It served him right.

"I assume you're okay with me staying here tonight?" Robert asked as Frankie tidied away the plates and glasses whilst he moved to the settee and repositioned the now slightly less than frozen peas against his face once again.

"You are welcome to sleep in the spare room," Frankie replied, inwardly cursing her naivety at believing Robert would want to stay somewhere else.

Robert said nothing for a few minutes, and Frankie didn't notice anyway, as she washed up the few bits they'd used and wrapped the leftover pizza to go in the fridge. However, by the time she was finished and came in to sit down, it was apparent to her that Robert wasn't happy. Again.

"What now?" she asked, unashamed to admit she was feeling a little less than patient with Robert after everything that had happened.

"Why do I have to sleep in the spare room?"

"Are you kidding me?"

Robert sighed. "I don't see why, after seven years together, I have to sleep in the spare room."

Frankie stood up and began to pace. "Have you lost your mind, Robert? Did Charlie cause some concussion when he punched you? Why would I let you sleep in my bed? Why? Don't you remember the last night we spent in our house, have you forgotten I slept in the spare room after that horrible row? Why, after you showed me up in front of my new friends and insulted Charlie the way you did, would I want you to sleep in my bed with me tonight?"

Robert couldn't believe the difference in the woman that stood before him. Compared to the Frankie he had lived with, the Frankie he had been unfaithful to, this Frankie was a different person. This Frankie was setting the rules, taking none of his crap.

"If I can't sleep next to you, I will go and stay at the hotel. And I'm warning you, Frankie, this is not a step forward for us."

Frankie laughed. "A step forward! Robert, go to the hotel. Let's hope they'll let you in with that bruise on your face. Go to the hotel, sleep on everything that's happened and let's talk again tomorrow when perhaps you'll feel a bit more circumspect about our relationship and your role in it."

Without another word, Robert stood, picked up his jacket and keys and walked out into the pouring rain, leaving the front door wide open as he did so. As Frankie closed the door, she heard his car engine as he roared up the hill and into the hotel car park.

Pouring herself a whiskey, Frankie turned off all the lights and sat in her favourite chair, watching the lightning as it lit up the bay.

Chapter 13

Sunday dawned, and Frankie stretched out in her warm and cosy bed. For a few moments, she had no cares in the world. Birds sang merrily in the trees outside her window, and the sun was shining. Bliss.

Without checking the time, she got up, unwilling to lie there and chew over every detail of Robert's visit and preferring instead to seize the day and face whatever it brought. Pushing her feet into her fluffy slippers and pulling on her dressing gown, she walked into the living room and opened the curtains before going to the kitchen to make a coffee.

As she stood by the kitchen sink waiting for the kettle to boil, she spotted Charlie in the distance across the field, walking with his two beloved dogs as they herded the sheep into a pen. Although he was far away, Frankie could tell he was sad. Something about his demeanour, how he stood, and how he moved - she knew him well enough to recognise when he struggled. However, in the days they had spent working on the cottage together over the last few weeks, he had shared little about Katie or his grief, beyond that one day, in the storm, when he told her about his guilt and not being there in the days before she died. Since that day, he had said little more, and as the kettle finally reached boiling point,

Frankie quietly acknowledged that she had shared little more with him either.

Grabbing a packet of digestive biscuits as she passed, Frankie went back into the warmth and comfort of the living room and settled herself down under the crochet blanket she had come to love so much. In the silence, her mind began to work through everything from last night, finally acknowledging the unwelcome reality that Robert was at the hotel and expecting to see Frankie again this morning for another talk. As far as she was concerned, there was little more to say to each other. He was refusing to see any error on his part, and she was becoming increasingly clear that the apology was his alone to make. If being so far away and cut off from him had proved one thing, it was that the fault for the breakdown in their relationship was his and that Frankie need feel no remorse at all. It was a liberating realisation, and to celebrate, Frankie dunked a bonus digestive into her coffee.

By 9.30, it was clear that Robert wasn't coming down to talk to her, so Frankie made the reluctant decision to walk up to the hotel and find him. Without any enthusiasm, and despite the beautiful sunny day, Frankie felt relatively subdued as she walked through the hotel gates and passed the car park. She scanned it for Robert's car but couldn't see it easily - there were several black saloons and knowing which one was his was impossible.

When she walked into reception, it was deserted, so she walked into the bar in the hope of finding Sue or Pete.

"Good morning, Frankie love. How are you after last night? Pete told me all about it. You poor thing. We were worried sick about you afterwards," said Sue, appearing from behind the bar and making Frankie jump.

"Thanks, Sue. It was kind of Pete to come down and help. I don't know what got into Robert. He's not usually like that...." She trailed off, disinclined to defend Robert to any great extent. She scanned the restaurant. "Has he already had breakfast? I wondered if I might catch him while he was eating."

"He didn't have breakfast, love. He checked out early this morning."

Pete walked in and joined the two women at the bar. "Looked pretty sheepish, if you ask me. His face was black and blue too. He was gone before we even started serving breakfast."

"Did he leave me any message?" asked Frankie, unsure whether she wanted to receive it if he had.

"Nothing. He barely spoke a word to me either. He just handed in his key, signed the bill and left. Are you two still together then?" Pete's curiously finally got the better of him.

"Pete! That's none of our business!" cried Sue, nudging Pete's shoulder. "Leave the poor girl alone. She's had enough bother this week without you giving her the third degree! She's got tonight off to relax after all that hassle, so at least let the girl try and forget about him and enjoy herself!"

"It's fine, Sue," Frankie said quickly. "It's complicated, Pete. I left him and told him I would give some thought to our relationship and what I wanted. He hurt me, and I needed some time to come to terms with that. This is the first time we've seen each other since I left in January...."

"Well, if you ask me, the man is unhinged, and you're better off without him!" said Pete, earning him an exasperated glare from Sue. "And if ditching him means you stay in Bayscar, I say ditch him!"

Sue rolled her eyes. "I'm sorry, Frankie, love. It's none of our business." She turned and looked directly at Pete. "Is it Peter?"

"I'm just saying...." Pete replied with a little less enthusiasm.

"I'll keep it in mind, Pete. Thanks though. For last night and everything."

"No thanks necessary, love. You're one of us now. We look after our own."

Leaving the hotel car park, Frankie decided to go for a walk and enjoy the day, especially now she knew Robert wouldn't be around to spoil it in any way. Instead of walking in the direction of the golf course and towards Charlie's farm and her favourite spot, she turned right and followed the road into the village, past Lilly's flat and then turned down a narrow lane that took her to the cliff edge and the coastal path.

This was a new route, and the path ran much closer to the cliff's edge than she was used to. It was exhilarating as she picked her way carefully along the narrow path, edged by nettles and long grass. There was less than a metre between her feet and the cliff edge, and it felt as though the sea were sucking her over the edge. Fortunately, the path opened up and became wider as she walked beyond the end of the village and into open country. There was no one around, and the silence was broken only by the gulls overhead and the sound of the strong breeze as it rushed past her ears.

After walking for almost half an hour, Frankie came to a strange derelict building, which looked military and extremely forbidding, with large unglazed windows and barbed wire on its roof. Intrigued by its location, Frankie stepped inside and found herself in a dark, damp space a million miles away from the bright sunshine outside. Graffiti covered the walls, some of it dating back decades, and there was rubbish strewn about the floor - empty drink cans and bottles, cigarette butts and empty food containers. As she stepped out the other side and back out into the fresh air, she found a board that explained the building was built in World

War 2 as an observation tower and fell into disuse in the 1950s when the military no longer required it. As she walked inland, in search of a less dangerous route back to the village, and with the strange building at her back, it occurred to Frankie that the men and women who worked there in the 1940s would be entertained to know the building was now a meeting place for bored teenagers, all these decades later.

At the far side of the field, Frankie found a nice wide track that pointed in the right direction, and she set off back towards Bayscar. The path was lined with a hedgerow that teemed with life, tiny birds flitting backwards and forwards, chirping constantly. To Frankie's delight, two or three robins popped out of the bushes and sang as she walked past, reminding her of her grandfather, who was convinced that if a robin came and said hello, it was someone you had lost letting you know they were nearby. Frankie wasn't convinced about the logic, but the robins were a welcome sight no matter what they signified.

As Bayscar came into sight, the hedgerow dropped down, and a small field came into view and clustered together in the farthest corner was a collection of animals, the like of which Frankie had never seen before. The closest Frankie could guess with long necks and fluffy bodies was that they were Llamas, but she wasn't sure. Luckily, a lady walked out and smiled as she walked past the house, allowing Frankie to ask.

"They're alpacas," explained the woman. "I keep them for their wool. And because they are adorable, of course!"

"They are the cutest things!" said Frankie, transfixed as she watched the quirky animals walk towards their owner.

"Come and meet them if you like?"

Frankie didn't hesitate, walking over and gingerly stroking the fluffy heads as they struggled to get close to their owner in the hope of getting fed.

"They're greedy little monkeys! I only fed them a couple of

hours ago!"

"Well, I think they are just gorgeous. Thank you for letting me meet them."

"Anytime," said the woman. "I'm Linda, by the way. Feel free to stop by again if you're passing."

"Thanks! I will. Oh, and I'm Frankie."

By the time Frankie got back to the village, it was lunchtime, and she was ravenous and thirsty and keen to get home. As she walked past the hotel, she saw something moving and realised it was one of Charlie's dogs. Frankie scanned the area to find Charlie, but he wasn't around. Realising she needed to get the dog back to Charlie somehow, and without any real plan or dog lead to hand, Frankie approached the dog and called out the name Zeus. There was no response, so she tried Sasha, and the dog looked up.

"Come here, Sasha. Come on!"

The dog walked over to Frankie with its tail wagging, and she fussed it, hoping to create some kind of bond, sufficient that Sasha might follow her down the track. Sasha caught the scent of alpacas on Frankie's hand and started to sniff vigorously. Seizing the opportunity, Frankie held her hand a few inches from Sacha's face and began to walk towards the track, and to her huge relief, Sasha followed her all the way down the track and into Charlie's yard.

"Charlie!" Frankie called, hoping that he would be home and able to take Sasha inside.

The door opened, and Charlie stepped outside, looking confused.

"I found Sasha up at the hotel," explained Frankie as Sasha ran over to Charlie and sat obediently next to his legs like butter wouldn't melt

"Honestly! She's been a little monkey just recently. Thank you so much." He ruffled Sasha's fur, and she nuzzled his hand before running inside the cottage to join Zeus. "Would you like to come in for a drink? It's the least I can do...."

Frankie was taken aback by the invitation, suddenly realising that although Charlie had spent many hours, days even, in the cottage, she had never set one foot in the farmhouse.

"Okay, just for a bit, though. I need to get back...." She had no need to get back and no clue why she said it, beyond hunger.

Charlie turned and walked inside, and Frankie followed, her eyes adjusting to the darkness as she moved further into the old building. Inside, there seemed to be a warren of doors and corridors, low ceilings and beautiful flagstone flooring. There were boots thrown by the front door, and Charlie's heavy coats were hung nearby. As she followed him through to the kitchen, she passed what must have been the living room, with an enormous open fireplace and a deep burgundy leather suite that looked worn and comfortable.

The kitchen was exquisite, with handmade oak cabinets and an old Rayburn oven. It was clearly the heart of Charlie's home, with a large table and chairs and a big old sofa, covered in a throw that looked out on the small garden beyond the patio doors. There were jars of spices on a shelf and bottles of wine, dusty in their rack.

"Have a seat," said Charlie pulling out a chair at the table. "I'd say you could sit on the sofa, but that's where the dogs like to sit at the moment, so it's not the best place for us."

Frankie sat down, and Charlie set about making a hot drink. "Do you want tea or coffee?"

"Coffee would be lovely, thanks. I've just walked to that World War 2 tower and back. It was lovely but quite a long way!"

"That's is a long way! You must be exhausted! And then you've walked down here to drop Sasha off. I'm so sorry about that. She's a little minx!"

"She's gorgeous, and it's fine. I'm just glad I found her."

"Well, I'm grateful. I couldn't bear to lose her. She was Katie's dog…."

"I thought as much," Frankie replied, unsure what else to say.

They made light chit chat for a while, both clearly making a deliberate effort to steer clear of discussing Robert's behaviour. Instead, Frankie talked about the alpaca farm she'd come across. Unfortunately, despite a solid effort, she could not persuade Charlie to branch out into alpaca farming, and he remained resolute in his determination to keep to sheep and cows. The time passed quickly, and Frankie's stomach began to rumble, the digestives long since burned up.

"Do you want something to eat?" Charlie asked, smiling as Frankie's stomach let out another loud call for food.

"No, it's fine. I should probably go. I have things I need to get done today," she lied.

As she went to stand up, there was a knock at the front door, and the dogs began to bark loudly, jumping off the sofa and running to the front door before Charlie could stop them.

"Sasha! Zeus! Enough!" he shouted as the dogs bolted past him. "I'll be back in a minute."

Frankie listened as the dogs, now shut in the living room, whimpered, and a muffled conversation took place in the hallway. After no more than a minute, there were footsteps, and Lilly walked into the kitchen.

"Frankie! Hey, you! What are you doing here?"

"She brought Sasha back," Charlie interjected quickly before Frankie could get a word in. "We were just having a coffee."

Lilly looked at Charlie and then at Frankie, her face reflecting the same confusion that Frankie felt. Charlie was being nervy and weird all of a sudden.

"I'm just going," said Frankie, keen to defuse the awkwardness.

"Oh, no need to leave on my account," said Lilly. "I only came to pick up the jumper I left when I rushed off yesterday morning. Is it in the other room?" she asked Charlie, who simply nodded.

Lilly left the room and then returned, clutching her jumper and being pestered by the dogs, now free to shower Lilly with affection.

"Right, I'm going!" said Frankie, far too brightly. "Thanks for the coffee."

"I'll show you out," said Charlie, opening the back door and letting the dogs into the garden so they would stop pestering Lilly.

"No, it's fine. You two chat, or whatever. I'll see myself out."

Frankie walked quickly from the kitchen, out the front door, and into the sunshine without another word. She couldn't get back to the cottage quickly enough, her cheeks blazing with embarrassment, anger and humiliation. Charlie and Lilly were together, and it was too much to take in.

As she closed the front door, she broke down in tears. Without taking off her shoes, she ran into the bedroom, threw herself on the bed and allowed herself to cry and cry. Without any conscious effort, all of the anger she felt about Robert, the fight, and how he had treated her came tumbling out as tears. All of the humiliation she felt for being so jealous of Lilly, so pathetic in her need for Charlie's kindness, and so alone in a world where Lilly and Charlie were together poured out as she sobbed into her pillow.

It was a mess, a big emotional tangle of a mess. And a mess Frankie had no emotional energy left to untangle.

As if he could sense that Frankie was in a low enough place to receive his message, Robert tapped out the text he had spent the entire drive home trying to get right. After his behaviour last night and the humiliation of asking that awful man with the bald head for a room in his crumby hotel, knowing he was the farmer's friend, it was fair to say Robert had had a bellyful of that village and the people in it.

But seeing Frankie again, seeing how she had grown in confidence and strength, how she stood up to him and made him leave her cottage rather than compromise herself; now that was a woman he could desire and respect. That was a woman he could be faithful to. It had taken him all night and a long journey down the motorway to realise it, but coming home to an empty house, and knowing Frankie was miles away, had hammered the point home. He would not stand aside and let that farmer take his woman. Charlie might have the looks, but there was a lot of history between Frankie and Robert. Seven years of history and shared experience that Charlie just could not bring to the table.

Robert's confidence was high. They had reconnected on that bench, watching the sea and lost in their memories of life together. He had seen the flicker of reconnection in her eyes, and were it not for that farmer busting in and ruining everything, they would be back together again now.

Robert sipped his whiskey, sitting back and holding the ice pack to his bruised face. It was only a matter of time until they were together again, until she was here, next to him, back where she belonged. He knew what she wanted, and he was finally ready to give it to her.

On a bed, two hundred fifty miles away, in a cottage perched high on the edge of a cliff, a phone lit up with a new message. Frankie opened her puffy eyes, picked up the phone from where she had thrown it down just moments ago, and stared at the screen.

Frankie. I am so genuinely sorry. I am sorry for last night, for fighting, for embarrassing you and for assuming I could sleep in your bed. But I'm also truly sorry for the hurt I've caused you, for the infidelity, for the lack of care and attention, the lack of respect and the lack of love. I know now that I love you, Frankie. I love you more than I can ever tell you. I love you and miss you, and I want you to come home. I want to try again. And I want you to know I WILL be better for you. I love you. R xx

Frankie read the message several times, unable to believe what she saw and trying to figure out what she wanted to say in response. It didn't take long, and without agonising over a single word, Frankie punched out her response and hit send.

I'll think about it.

Chapter 14

In the aftermath of Robert's text message and the embarrassing encounter at Charlie's house with Lilly, Frankie felt like her mind was a mess. On the one hand, she was pleased that Charlie and Lilly were together if it made them happy, and it certainly seemed to do that. But on the other hand, there was a persistent whisper of envy that Frankie couldn't silence. And the text from Robert just made everything a million times more complicated!

Charlie was a wonderful man, of that Frankie had no doubt. And he was good looking and kind and had a rare emotional quality that Robert didn't possess. It would be so easy to fall for someone like Charlie, obviously. But Frankie wasn't looking for love, or even a fling, so the envy didn't make sense, and it wasn't welcome. Not while Robert was still in the picture. And he was.

Robert had been her partner for so many years. Every time Frankie tried to close her heart and mind to Robert, all of their history seemed to rise and wedge it open a little. They had built a life together, and although it was easier to remember the bad things, the affairs and the lack of remorse, there had been some lovely times. Weekends away and holidays in the sun, Frankie had even persuaded Robert to go on a Nile cruise! And they'd had a wonderful time. They had been good together once. Once, and perhaps there was still hope they could be good together again. It was hard to let those thoughts go.

With so much emotional turmoil to work through, Frankie maintained a low profile in the days that followed. She worked her shifts at the hotel but slipped away at the end of each one, using the side entrance to the restaurant and missing the bar altogether. When her path had crossed with Lilly, the conversation was light and friendly, and yet, Frankie no longer felt comfortable in Lilly's company. Worse still, she felt lousy about it, months of friendship threatened by a whisper of discomfort.

She hadn't seen Charlie all week, and the relief she felt was palpable, having decided that she didn't have any real feelings for him beyond a pathetic need of his kindness. But the lack of contact between them could never last forever. The annual village fete was on the horizon, and everyone had their part to play. Frankie was running the cake stall, and so any hope of continuing to avoid Charlie was virtually nil. Sure enough, about an hour after the mayor declared the Bayscar Village Fete open, Charlie made his way through the crowd towards the stall, the cakes and Frankie.

"Hey, you! Have you been avoiding me?"

Frankie blushed furiously at the question. "No! Why would I do that? I've just been busy. Had a lot on my mind after Robert's visit."

"I'm just kidding, Frankie! I was just a bit worried that I hadn't seen you all week, that's all. As long as you're okay?"

"Yeah, I'm fine. Just a lot going on…" she ran out of words, the lie not exactly rolling off the tongue.

"Have you heard from Robert since he went back down south?" Charlie asked, handing over some cash to pay for the ginger cake he'd just picked up.

"He sent me a text on Sunday. He wants me back. Says

he'll change," Frankie replied, handing him his change and trying to sound as relaxed as possible.

"And do you believe him? Is that what you want?" Charlie asked, raising an eyebrow.

They locked eyes for a moment, Charlie's eyes piercing straight into Frankie's soul, leaving her feeling exposed. She looked away quickly.

"I said I'll think about it. That's all. And I will."

"Fair enough. You have to do what's right for you," Charlie replied, looking far less convinced than his words might indicate, baffled by Frankie's apparent inclination to give Robert any thought at all.

An older couple approached the stall and began to ask Frankie if she had any gluten and dairy-free cakes, and by the time Frankie had finished helping them, Charlie had disappeared into the crowd.

It was a wonderful occasion, sponsored by the hotel every year to raise money for charity The garden was decorated with bunting, there was a band playing, and people from neighbouring villages brought their wares along to bolster the offerings from Bayscar itself. The afternoon passed quickly, and once she relaxed, Frankie found she was enjoying herself, chatting to the villagers and exploring the different stalls during her break. She was particularly excited to see Linda, the alpaca farmer at her own stall, and admired the gorgeous jumpers and scarves - so much so that she bought a scarf in readiness for the winter.

As she walked back to the cake stall, stroking the soft scarf in her hand, she wondered whether she would still be in Bayscar for the coming winter. The question hung in her mind, unanswered. She still needed to get back to Robert. It was unfair to leave him hanging on after such an explicit declaration of intent, and she felt guilty that a week had passed already with no word from her. But despite having plenty of time to think about what she wanted, especially since she was avoiding her two closest friends, Frankie still couldn't decide what to do. And until she did know what to do, Robert would have to wait.

As the crowd began to disperse and the fete was packed away for another year, many people moved into the hotel bar and continued the festivities inside. Frankie planned to head home, but Charlie had other ideas and steered her towards the hotel bar. As they walked in, she saw Lilly waving furiously from a table she was sharing with Tash and a couple of others. Reluctantly, Frankie sat down, resolving to stay for one or two drinks and then slip away.

"What's everyone having?" asked Charlie before heading to the bar with a long list.

"This is Annabel!" Lilly shouted across the table to Frankie whilst pointing at one of the faces Frankie didn't recognise.

"Hi!" Frankie shouted at Annabel, ensuring she was heard over all the noise.

Annabel smiled warmly, and Frankie liked her immediately. There was something about her that seemed friendly and welcoming. She was petite, achingly stylish and her hair was an indefinable colour, with shades of red, brown, blonde. In short, Annabel was gorgeous, and once again, Frankie felt the familiar feeling of being a little dowdy in comparison.

"You okay?" Charlie asked as he handed out the drinks and eased himself into a seat next to Frankie, watching her as she assessed Annabel.

"Yep. Annabel's pretty, isn't she?"

Charlie looked at Annabel and then back at Frankie, a mischievous smile dancing on his lips. "She's not as pretty as you if you ask me."

Frankie couldn't believe what Charlie had said, and

Charlie seemed a little surprised too because he stood again quickly and without warning and left the table. Frankie thought she could see his cheeks flushed red, but he moved at such a pace she would never know for sure.

As the evening wore on, the bar became more and more noisy, full of young men who had travelled in from another village. Behind the bar, Pete looked a little agitated, and eventually, Sue abandoned her post at reception to give him a hand. The event had been an enormous success for the hotel and the charity that would benefit from the proceeds of the fete, but everyone was starting to feel exhausted. On the other hand, the young men seemed to be having a great time. Cheers and laughter erupted regularly, rendering conversation virtually impossible.

Frankie and Lilly attempted a conversation despite the noise, huddling together, so they didn't need to shout.

"Where do I know Annabel from?" Frankie asked. She had seen Annabel somewhere before, but she couldn't figure out where or when for the life of her.

"She was a bridesmaid at that wedding we did a few weeks ago! Don't you remember? She pulled me up to dance to that ABBA song…."

"Oh yeah! I remember now. I didn't realise you'd stayed in touch! She seems really nice."

"She is. We get on really well," said Lilly, reaching for her drink. "That reminds me, I haven't had a chance to ask you. So what's the deal with you and Robert now?"

Frankie pulled a face, and Lilly laughed. "That good, eh?"

"Honestly, Lilly. I don't know what to do. He says he will change and that he loves me. He even told me he's sorry, for heaven's sake. What am I supposed to do with that?" Frankie sounded every bit as exasperated as she felt. As she waited for Lilly's response, she realised what an idiot she had been, keeping away from Lilly because of her ridiculous and muddled up feelings for Charlie. She had missed her friend so much - and with everything she'd been through these past months, she needed Lilly's friendship.

"I know what I'd do with it," said Lilly, with a wicked look in her eye. "I'd tell him to shove his apology up his arse! You can do better than him, Frank! Seriously. There are much better men than him that would snap you up in a heartbeat!"

Frankie laughed. "They're not exactly queuing up, Lilly!" To emphasise the point, Frankie looked around and back at Lilly. "See, no one there."

"Just a room full of men. And Charlie, of course. So yeah, no one around. You weirdo! You're gorgeous - seriously. You would be single for about one bloody minute if you were seriously in the market for a guy!"

"Yeah, well, I'm not. So that's that." The last thing Frankie wanted was the complication of another man in her life until she had decided what to do about Robert, of that much she was certain.

"Where is Charlie anyway?" asked Lilly, standing up and looking around the room.

"I think he's behind the bar helping Pete and Sue."

Lilly stood on her tiptoes, and sure enough, there was Charlie, pulling a pint with a deep frown. He couldn't have looked any less impressed by the clientele if he'd tried. It was close to closing time, and the bar hadn't emptied at all. There was a steady stream of guys walking in and out for a smoke, beer bottles, and glasses left on every available surface through the bar and even in the reception area, and Sue was beginning to look very stressed by the whole thing.

"This is a quiet hotel, Peter. Not some town pub. Where have all these men come from?" she hissed as Pete walked past her to collect some glasses.

"I overheard one of them saying they're on some kind of pub crawl, and we're the last stop. I think a couple of minibuses are coming to collect them at 11."

Sue looked at her watch and shook her head. "This is not how my hotel bar is supposed to feel, Peter. Something bad is going to happen; I can feel it."

"Go upstairs and calm yourself down, Sue. Charlie and I can manage from here. It'll be fine. I promise you. Go on."

Sue didn't take much persuading and disappeared up the back stairs quickly.

As closing time approached, the bar thankfully began to empty a little, but the crowd of guys didn't budge, drinking as much as they could as quickly as they could before last orders were called.

"I need to go to the loo," Frankie said, standing up and easing herself out from behind the table. "See you in a minute."

Lilly watched as Frankie tried to pick her way through the crowd of guys, who moved to assemble in front of the toilets as soon as they saw Frankie approach. Lilly shot a look of dismay to Charlie, but it looked as though Frankie was okay. She walked confidently towards the men and asked them to move, which they did. She gave the impression of being un-phased by their presence, but Charlie and Lilly knew her well enough to know that she would be a quivering wreck inside.

Frankie disappeared through the door, and Lilly resumed her conversation with Annabel but kept one eye on the toilet door whilst Charlie returned to wiping the glasses as they came out of the dishwasher. A few minutes passed, and the bar seemed to quieten slightly, giving Pete cause to smile at Charlie, believing the worst might yet be over.

Frankie emerged from the toilet and began to walk through the group again. But this time, she didn't make it through.

"Come 'ere gorgeous." A sweaty, overweight twenty-something with ginger hair and a thin beard grabbed Frankie by the waist and pulled her towards him.

Frankie screamed, and Lilly jumped up. Charlie dropped his cloth and began moving out from behind the bar.

"Let her go NOW!" cried Lilly as she raced over and grabbed Frankie's arm to pull her away from her captor, as Frankie wriggled to get herself free.

But he held on tight to Frankie, and she couldn't get away, even with Lilly's help. The situation deteriorated quickly as another man in the group grabbed Lilly and twisted her arm backwards before throwing her to the ground and laughing at his friends. Lilly's head hit the corner of the bar as she fell, and she landed heavily and in obvious pain.

Annabel rushed over to comfort her, and Pete immediately stepped out from behind the bar, striding over to the group, followed closely by Charlie.

"Let go of her, please, or there'll be trouble," Pete said with more confidence than he felt.

"And what are you going to do about it, Grandad!" mocked a tall, muscular, tattoo-covered man, placing his pint down on a nearby table.

"He's not going to do anything. But I am..." Charlie's face was thunderous; his fists clenched tightly at his side.

The man holding Frankie drained of colour and let her go instantly, pushing her away and into Charlie's arms, and Charlie didn't let go, instead standing firm and staring hard at the group. "Pete, call the police."

The group shuffled awkwardly and looked at each other before moving quickly towards the door. The smell of beer and sweat was overpowering as they moved, and Frankie buried her head against Charlie's chest as he wrapped his arms around her, protecting her from any further physical intrusion.

Pete tried to block their exit as he dialled 999 but hung up quickly; once it was clear, he could not halt the retreating group. They didn't look back, leaving Pete with no option but to close the door and lock it, ensuring they couldn't come back in.

Charlie released Frankie but held her shoulders. "Are you okay? Did he hurt you?"

"I'm fine, really. But Lilly…." Her body was shaking, and she felt sick, but there was no physical damage. Lilly, however, looked to be in a bad way.

Charlie's attention immediately dropped to the floor where Lilly was lying, writhing in agony and being comforted by Annabel.

"I think we need an ambulance!" Annabel called out to anyone who would listen. "Can someone call? My phone is on the table over there."

"I'll call now," said Charlie, letting go of Frankie and turning from her quickly to check on Lilly, before pulling out his phone and marching back to the door to unlock it. He wanted to check that the men had all gone. They had.

Satisfied that the ambulance was on its way, Charlie came back in and sank to the floor next to Lilly. Annabel melted away and left them both on the floor together as Charlie stroked Lilly's hair and tried to keep her calm and distracted from the pain in her head and arm.

Left on her own as Charlie cared for Lily, Frankie made her way to the table and downed the dregs of her whiskey, and Pete rushed over with another. "Here, get this down you, love. You look like you need it."

The whole situation had unfolded so quickly it was almost surreal. The bar was quiet, and the only sound was Lilly crying gently and Charlie soothing her, and the occasional clink of a glass as Pete tidied up. Everyone listened out for the ambulance, but Bayscar was a good 20-minute drive from the nearest hospital, and it was Saturday night, so there was no telling how long it might take to arrive.

It took almost half an hour for the ambulance to get to the hotel, and the paramedics rushed through the front door, directed to Lilly by Sue, now back in the bar having been thoroughly disturbed by the noise of the unfolding drama. They worked on Lilly where she lay before rolling her carefully onto a stretcher and preparing her for transfer to the hospital. She had a suspected fracture and a likely concussion caused by a heavy blow to her head as she fell.

"I'll come with you," said Charlie as they manoeuvred Lilly onto the stretcher.

"What about the dogs?" Lilly asked.

"I'll go down and check on them tonight and first thing tomorrow, Charlie. You go with Lilly," said Pete, as Sue grabbed his hand and squeezed it.

"Thanks, mate," said Charlie, digging his keys from his pocket and throwing them over to Pete. "The front door key is the big one."

"Got it. Don't worry about a thing. I'll make sure they're okay," replied Pete, placing the keys in his pocket for safekeeping.

"Right, if everyone is ready, let's make a move," said one of the paramedics, and they began to carry Lilly out of the bar.

Frankie rushed over to Lilly and grabbed her hand as they neared the door. "Thank you, Lilly. For trying to help me. I'm so sorry this happened!" Tears spilt over, and Frankie stepped back.

"It wasn't your fault, Frank. I'll be okay, promise. Visit me. And bring chocolate!" And she was gone.

Charlie followed the paramedics out, and Pete closed the door behind them before everyone heaved a collective sigh of relief.

"Right, how is everyone getting home?" asked Sue, ever practical, even in her nightie and dressing gown.

"I've got my car, so I can give anyone a lift that needs

one?" said Annabel, and a couple of Lilly's friends accepted her offer.

"I only live down the track…" began Frankie, but Pete cut her off.

"I'm walking down that way to see Charlie's dogs, so I'll walk you back."

Frankie nodded gratefully. She was still shaky, and the idea of being alone out there in the dark wasn't comfortable at all.

Once she was back in the cottage, with the door locked and yet another whiskey in hand, Frankie began to work through the events of the evening. The horror of that man holding her against his torso was unbearable, the memory of his breath, the feel of his hands around her ribcage, his thumb pressing against her breast. She downed her drink in one, desperate to numb the feeling of violation and disgust.

Her thoughts moved to Charlie holding her, and she felt safe, enclosed in his arms, pulled tightly against his body. As much as she knew it was foolish to acknowledge it, she didn't want him to let her go. And yet he did - to help Lilly.

The whiskey was starting to take effect - she had drunk a fair amount of it in the last hour, that's for sure - and somewhere deep in her psyche, she knew that being annoyed that Charlie had let her go to look after Lilly was unreasonable. It was a courteous and decent thing to do. But the bigger part of her mind, the bit that was blissfully bathing in the effects of several whiskies, felt hurt, angry and aggrieved. How dare he hold her like that, let her feel his strength and the warmth of his body, the sound of his heart beating in his chest, the indescribable feeling of sanctuary. How dare he pull her so close, allow her to feel so much of his presence when the woman he truly wanted was Lilly.

Images of Charlie stroking Lilly's hair, holding her hand and soothing her, raced forward in Frankie's mind, and she shook her head and squeezed her eyes shut as if to block them out. But it didn't work, and even as the room began to sway, a small voice in Frankie's head was still coherent enough to whisper that she shouldn't care.

Frankie flopped down onto the settee, swinging her legs up and attempting to kick off her shoes, one of them flying across the room and landing next to the TV, the other remaining connected to her foot. She twisted and lay down, feeling like the room was spinning wildly. It wasn't a pleasant sensation.

"I've had far too much whisky, Grandma," she said aloud. "And I, really, really miss you…. you'd know what to do. You'd tell me what to say to Robert."

Frankie's face collapsed into a deep frown at the mention of Robert's name, and she began to laugh. The room carried on spinning, and she closed her eyes. With every light in the cottage left on, still wearing her jacket and one shoe, Frankie Gleane let out a big sigh, shouted that she loved her grandma at the top of her voice, turned onto her side and passed out.

Chapter 15

The sound of dogs barking ripped Frankie from her slumber, and as she opened her eyes, she clamped them closed again; the light streaming in from the windows and from the ceiling lamp directly above her proving unbearable. As she lay there, eyes firmly closed, Frankie did a quick body scan to assess the situation.

Her legs and arms felt fine, although she was only wearing one shoe, which didn't make much sense. Her back ached, and something was digging into her side, which on further investigation, turned out to be her phone, jammed into her jacket pocket. Her neck felt tight and painful, having been twisted in an awkward position all night. And then she came to her head. And what a poorly head! Dehydrated due to the vast quantity of whiskey she consumed late last night, Frankie's mouth was as dry as the Sahara Desert, and the pounding headache was a solid eight out of ten bad.

Overall, things couldn't have felt much worse, physically at least. And as Frankie ran through the events leading up to her spectacular collapse onto the settee, it seemed that emotionally things were also pretty dire. All of the lovely feelings she had when Charlie held her were still there, along with the jealousy and humiliation of Charlie's dash to Lilly's aid and the ever-present quandary of what to do about

Robert.

Realising that lying where she was all day was only going to make her feel worse - as impossible as that felt - Frankie eased herself upright, and the full impact of her dehydrated state hit her like a wall. With her eyes barely open, she was running on pure instinct as she gingerly moved into the kitchen, poured a large glass of cold tap water and glugged it back quickly before repeating the process. Rarely had water tasted so good.

She glanced at the digital clock on the oven and was shocked to see it was almost 10.30. Reaching for her phone, she checked her messages and found three from Lilly. The first was checking Frankie was okay, the second was letting Frankie know she was staying in overnight, and the last was a repeated plea for Frankie to visit ASAP and bring chocolate. A quick mental calculation told her she would be safe to drive in an hour and so, draining the last of the water, Frankie placed the glass next to the sink, switched on the kettle, grabbed a cereal bar and headed for the bathroom. A shower, a coffee and then off to the hospital, and all with the headache from hell.

Even though it was four months since Frankie moved to Yorkshire, she had driven very little. The journey to the hospital was fraught with narrow lanes and steep hills. That was before the complexity of navigating a town with which she was unfamiliar. Mercifully, on a Sunday morning, the traffic was very light, and the hospital was well signposted. Within half an hour, which included a pitstop at a corner shop for as much chocolate as Frankie could fit in her bag, she pulled into a parking space, reasonably close to the main entrance.

To speed the arrival of her chocolate, Lilly had texted Frankie the ward number and detailed instructions on how to find it, and Frankie quickly found herself pressing the buzzer to access the ward. As she walked in, she could hear Lilly laughing, and as a curtain was pulled back around, Lilly was revealed, lying in her bed, looking as glamourous as ever and giggling with a male nurse.

"Ah, here comes my chocolate!" cried Lilly expectantly as Frankie approached.

"Well, that's just charming! I might not give it to you now!" Frankie laughed.

"You know I love you, and I'm pleased to see you, but honestly, I need that chocolate! It's nothing personal, I promise!"

Frankie opened her bag and tipped a pile of chocolate bars onto Lilly's blanket, and Lilly's eyes widened like saucers. "You got me all this?"

"Well, all of that except one bar. So, whichever you like least is the one I'll have," Frankie replied, hoping Lilly wouldn't offer her the one with mint in it.

Lilly offered Frankie her pick, and Frankie stashed her chosen bar back in her bag for later. Unfortunately, the hangover wasn't entirely gone, and the idea of chocolate wasn't as appealing to Frankie as it apparently was for Lilly. She was ripping the wrapper with her teeth and enjoying her second bar already!

The ward was pleasant enough. Light and bright and freshly decorated by the looks of it. The walls were a soothing pale green, and the windows were big and hung with Venetian blinds so they could open and close to protect the patients from the sun. There were tasteful pictures dotted around and flowers at almost every bedside.

"I should have bought you some flowers!" Frankie said, feeling guilty.

"Don't worry. You got me chocolate," Lilly said, her mouth full of chocolate. "And Charlie will bring flowers when he gets here anyway."

Frankie could feel herself tense up and made a conscious effort to relax and push past it, instead chatting to Lilly about her arm, which was now set in a cast and suspended in a sling around her neck. Lilly explained that when she had been pushed to the floor, her arm had been twisted back by the guy that pushed her. The way she landed fractured her humerus, and she could look forward to being in her sling for upwards of three months.

Their conversation was interrupted by a nurse who came over and checked Lilly's chart before taking the empty water jug and replacing it with a fresh one from a trolley she was pushing from bed to bed. A young family rushed in and created a stir, with three small children running at a bed in the far corner of the room, where an emotional mother welcomed them with a look of intense joy. The children's father tried to calm them down before leaning in kissing the patient. It was a scene that tugged at Frankie's heart in a way she could sorely do without. Her longing for children hadn't diminished, and even though the dream of creating a large family with Robert now hung in the balance, Frankie's desire to be a mother still burned brightly within.

Ever perceptive, Lilly observed Frankie as she watched the young family; the longing in her eyes was unmistakable.

"Are you still planning to go to your dad's 70th birthday this week?" Lilly asked as Frankie turned away from the family at last.

"I think so, yes. I've swapped shifts with Byron, so that's all sorted. Dreading the drive down, mind you. It's such a long way to go."

Frankie had been invited to Martin's 70th a few weeks ago and was looking forward to seeing her parents and being back in Buckinghamshire for a couple of days. Jane had arranged a surprise party and invited all of Martin's family and friends, including Frankie. She smiled inwardly, remembering opening the envelope and thinking only her mum could actually invite her to her own dad's birthday party. It would be a big event and a chance for Frankie to catch up with everyone. And that was as much a blessing as a source of intense stress, the scrutiny of her relationship status a deeply unwelcome but unavoidable prospect.

"Will you see Robert?" Lilly asked, tackling the thorniest issue straight off the bat.

"Probably," Frankie replied without enthusiasm. "I doubt Mum will have invited him to the party, but I'll have to go and see him while I'm back. We need to talk, and I guess face to face is better than by text or phone call." Since the text exchange, Frankie had managed to avoid any further contact with Robert. He was giving her the space to think that she'd asked for, and Frankie was taking full advantage of it.

Lilly's phone lit up, and the conversation paused while she read the message, her frustration at having one usable arm clear to see.

"It's Charlie. He's coming now; he should be here soon." Lilly was beaming, and Frankie managed to smile too, although with marginally less conviction.

"He was amazing last night. The way he looked after you and came with you in the ambulance...."

"Charlie is always amazing," Lilly said dreamily. "He's my hero."

"He was certainly your hero last night," Frankie agreed. "And mine. He stood up to that guy and got me away from him...." The memory of Charlie's arms wrapped around her and the heat of his body washed over her again, and it was an unwelcome intrusion which Lilly's continuing conversation quickly banished.

"He has taken such great care of me since I arrived. I would be lost without him. Honestly, Frank, that man is everything to me. The closest thing I have to family. I don't know how I ever lived a day of my life without him in it." Lilly's eyes filled with tears, and Frankie reached for a tissue from the unit next to the bed, passing it to Lilly's free hand. "Sorry. I don't know why I'm so emotional. Maybe I'm just tired…."

"You must be exhausted. Would you like me to leave you to it?"

"No! I'll be bored to tears, and Charlie might be ages. Tell me about Robert. What are you going to say to him? Have you decided yet?"

Frankie closed her eyes and tried to work out what she would say to Robert. It was so complicated. Robert wanted her back, and she needed to explore that, to understand what he was proposing and whether it was what she wanted. But equally, no matter how much she loved Lilly, she was attracted to Charlie, and after last night, it was pointless denying it.

"It's complicated. I'll talk to him. See what he wants," Frankie replied at last.

"It doesn't seem that complicated to me, Frankie. And as I technically have a head injury, I'm going to be honest with you, okay? And if you don't like what I say, we can just chalk it up to the concussion and forget all about it? Are you okay with that?"

Frankie smiled at her friend. Lilly was so opinionated anyway; she didn't need a head injury to justify what she was about to say. She nodded, and Lilly shifted position and adopted a serious expression.

"Right. As I see it, you came up here to get away from Robert because you needed some time to think. You needed the time to think because he is a prolific womaniser who has repeatedly been unfaithful to you, and you decided back in January that you'd had enough. In the four months since, he's only been up to see you once, he made a scene and humiliated you in front of your friends and then slunk back into his hole before facing you. You have built a nice life in Bayscar. You are one of us now. If you go back to him, you go back down there. We lose you, and you lose us! None of us wants you to go - none of us. We would all miss you. I would miss you, Frankie!"

The children in the corner let out a shriek, disturbing Lilly's big speech, but undeterred, she took a sip of her drink and continued. "You're still thinking about going back to him, so you obviously have feelings for him, although God knows why! You obviously still care for him, so you have to go down there and see what's left between you. I get it. I really do. But when you're down there, Frank, look at him properly, don't take any crap from him, and if it feels even the slightest bit wrong, you haul ass and get back up here where you belong. Right? Do we have a deal?"

Frankie was taken aback by the force of Lilly's feelings about her situation. Hearing Lilly's take on Robert and their relationship gave a completely fresh perspective on it. She did need to go down there and talk to Robert because - and Lilly had hit the nail on the head - at no point so far had Frankie been able to draw a line and say no, enough, I don't love you anymore. Robert was still an issue that needed tackling.

"Thank you, Lilly. I needed to hear all of that. Every word of it."

"Oh! Wow! In that case, it wasn't my concussion talking. It was me, and I meant it all. But just so you know, I really want you to come back, okay?"

"I know you do. And I love you for it," Frankie replied, meaning every word.

Frankie made her way down the stairs and through the

network of poorly signposted corridors until she found the exit. The hospital reception was busier now than when she arrived, and Frankie picked her way carefully through the crowd and headed for the main doors.

"Frankie!"

Frankie turned towards the voice and spotted Charlie, standing on the other side of a small group of women and children. He was holding a bouquet, and Frankie smiled to herself. Lilly was absolutely right; he had brought flowers, and not just a bunch from the local garage, a rather lovely bouquet. She made her way over to Charlie's side of the group, and they moved to one side to prevent any further hold-ups for the people milling in and out.

"Are you leaving?" he asked, somewhat unnecessarily as Frankie had been heading towards the exit when he called her.

Rather than point out the screamingly obvious, Frankie nodded.

"How's Lilly doing? Is she okay?"

"She's fine. Doing well, I'd say. I brought her a lot of chocolate, so she's happily working her way through that. And she's looking forward to seeing you. What time did you get home last night?"

"The taxi dropped me back at the house at about two, I think. I let Pete know I was back and not to worry about the dogs. He left my keys in the barn and texted me, so I could get in if I arrived home overnight."

"Pete is so lovely. Everyone is. I love it in Bayscar," said Frankie, reflecting on her conversation with Lilly.

"Do you fancy grabbing a coffee before I go up? I'm sure Lilly won't mind waiting a bit longer…."

Frankie wasn't sure whether to say yes, still wrestling with the extraordinarily awkward but decidedly pleasant memory of Charlie holding her tight. Without thinking, she blurted out, "Yes."

"Great. The cafe is this way. Follow me. How's work on the cottage going?"

Frankie was relieved that the conversation was focused on a safe and neutral subject. "Pretty good. I need to sort out the decking behind the bedroom, and then it's in good enough shape."

"Good enough shape for what?" asked Charlie, pushing open the cafe door and letting Frankie walk through.

"I don't know. Live in, sell. I guess it depends on what I decide to do...."

Charlie didn't reply, and Frankie thought little of it, walking into the cafe and looking for a free table, spotting one near the window and making a beeline before anyone else got there first. They sat down. Charlie left the flowers with Frankie and went to get a couple of coffees. As he walked over to the counter, Frankie checked her phone. There was a message from Robert, asking if she was coming down for Martin's birthday. She punched out a quick response and stuffed the phone back into her pocket as Charlie sat back down.

"Everything okay?" he asked, noting Frankie's mild irritation.

"Oh, just a text from Robert asking if I'm going home for Dad's birthday this week."

"You're going home?" This was the first Charlie had heard of it.

"Yeah. For a couple of days, maybe longer. I don't know. Mum's throwing a big party for Dad's 70th, and I guess I'll go and see Robert while I'm down there."

Charlie sipped his coffee and immediately regretted it, burning his tongue, and they sat in awkward silence for a few moments. Frankie looked around the cafe and watched people as they came and went. Hospitals were places of such joy and profound sadness and every emotion in between. The customers in the cafe were a perfect cross-section of the emotional range. People were laughing, people were crying, and people were deep in conversation. There were angry phone calls and joyful ones too. The entire gamut of human experience all squeezed into one characterless, sterile hospital cafe.

"Lilly is excited to see you," Frankie said, breaking their silence.

"Lilly is excited to see everyone. She's full of goodness and kindness. There's a special kind of joy in Lilly's heart that is rare...." Charlie drifted into silence, an inexplicable melancholy settling on him without warning.

Frankie tried to piece it all together, and suddenly everything made sense. Charlie and Lilly weren't together. The idea had never sat comfortably because Charlie was still wearing his wedding ring. But he was in love with Lilly. It was so obvious now. How did she not see this before? The way he spoke about Lilly was reminiscent of how he talked about Katie. With the same tenderness.

As if a dam had burst, the whole situation exploded into clarity. Charlie loved Lilly; Lilly loved Charlie, and all that stood between them was the memory of Katie. But if the way they spoke about each other was any indication, it would take little more to bring them together.

"Are you okay?" Charlie asked, concerned that Frankie had gone so quiet after his compliments towards Lilly. "Have I said something to upset you?"

Frankie felt like the world was shifting beneath her feet, her foundations shaken. The brilliant clarity that Charlie and Lilly were meant to be together was incredible; she was thrilled for them both, her dearest friends in Bayscar. Her dearest friends, period. Anything she felt for Charlie - and she wasn't even sure what she felt - was pointless. It was wasted, and it was wrong. Charlie and Lily would do anything for Frankie, and she had seen that loyalty and dedication time and time again in the short time she had been their friend. The very least she could do was be pleased for them, give them her love and support, and be there for them as they navigate their future together.

It was Frankie's turn to burn herself on the coffee in her haste to appear busy. "I'm fine. Sorry. I didn't mean to unsettle you. I was just thinking about Robert."

"Do you think you'll get back together?" Charlie asked quietly as he played with his wedding ring.

"I'll go down there and talk to him. I need to hear what he has to say."

Frankie watched Charlie as he processed the idea of her talking to Robert, puzzled by his apparent discomfort with the idea. He frowned and took off his ring, rolling it between his fingers like a coin.

"I've been thinking about not wearing this anymore," Charlie said out of the blue, placing the ring in the palm of his hand and showing it to Frankie. She could see the ring was engraved inside, and there were scratch marks and scuffs on the outer rim.

"It's a big decision to make, Charlie. But only you can make it. You'll know when the time is right."

"We both have some big decisions to make, don't we? Me and this ring; you and Robert. We are both at a turning point, it seems...."

Their eyes met for a moment, but Frankie looked away quickly, unable to keep her emotions in check unless she was brutally careful from this point on. Charlie was all but telling her he was ready for a life with Lilly. Appearing upbeat and prepared for a life with Robert was essential if Frankie was going to walk out of here with any dignity.

"We do," Frankie said in her perkiest, most cheerful voice.

"And I think we'll both be fine. Now, don't you think you should go up and visit Lilly before she sends out a search party?"

Charlie looked at Frankie as she finished her coffee and did her very best impression of someone on the cusp of an exciting new life. He sighed, unable to match Frankie's enthusiasm for the future. The contrast between their attitudes seemingly a gaping abyss in his eyes, at least.

"I'm not visiting Lilly. I'm here to bring her home," Charlie explained.

"Oh! I could have done that! Saved you the journey…."

"It's no bother, and I'm not dropping her off at her flat anyway. She's coming to live with me. She can't look after herself with her arm in that sling, so I've said she can move in for a bit."

Frankie was speechless, nodding and smiling but lost for words. Everything made sense now. Charlie was ready to take off his wedding ring, and Lilly was moving in. She should be happy for them. And of course, she would be happy for them once she'd had the chance to wrap her head around the idea of them as a couple and banish the ridiculous memories of Charlie holding her last night. But right now, she needed to get the hell out of this cafe and away from Bayscar.

"Right. Well, I'd better get going then! I'll see you when I'm back from Mum and Dad's," Frankie said, the light and airy tone she was aiming for sounding somewhat tight and slightly high pitched instead.

Before Charlie could say another word, Frankie turned on her heel and walked out of the cafe.

Confounded by how Frankie left their conversation, Charlie had no choice but to pick up his flowers and navigate the warren of corridors and stairs until he found Lilly's ward. As he walked, in no particular hurry, he tried to figure out what made Frankie run away. Perhaps she was uncomfortable talking about Robert with him after what had happened that night when Robert had caused such a terrible scene? Since it happened, Frankie had been avoiding him, and apart from a quick chat at the fete and a few words in the hotel bar last night, they hadn't talked about it in any detail.

Remembering last night, the memory of holding Frankie in his arms surged forward, not entirely unwelcome. She had been shaking, so afraid, and he held her tight to make her feel safe. Perhaps he had scared her with his need to protect her? She was so fragile, all he wanted to do was keep her safe, but maybe it was too much?

The ward door buzzed open, and Charlie strolled in to find Lilly sitting on the edge of her bed, all dressed and ready to go. Her arm was in a sling, and in the bin next to her bed were more chocolate wrappers than any person should discard in a week, let alone an hour!

"What on earth has happened to you?" cried Lilly as he approached the bed.

"Shouldn't I be asking you that?" Charlie replied, smiling.

"I'm serious. Something's happened. What is it? Tell me?"

"I've just seen Frankie. We had a coffee…."

"Okay. Tell me all about it," said Lilly, patting the bed for him to sit down. "And thanks for the flowers, by the way."

Charlie smiled and sat down. If there was one person in the world he could talk to about this, it was Lilly.

Chapter 16

Jane Gleane opened her front door and took in the sight before her eyes; her beautiful daughter had arrived two days earlier than planned and looked radiant and healthy. The time in Yorkshire had undoubtedly done her a world of good, but even so, a mother knows her daughter, and it was clear to see that something was still amiss. There was a certain sadness in her eyes that her chirpy demeanour couldn't hide. It was a disappointment, but one Jane would brush under the proverbial carpet for the time being. The last four months had been burdensome, missing her daughter more than she could ever have imagined. And so, the priority was to throw her arms around her precious girl and cuddle her. Everything else could wait.

Martin appeared at Jane's side and, after hugging Frankie, picked up her bags and carried them into the house, walking behind the two women as they moved into the kitchen. In anticipation of Frankie's arrival, Jane had gone into town and bought almost everything she could lay her hands on that Frankie might enjoy. To Martin's delight, the fridge and cupboards were bursting with every kind of delicious foodstuff. Although he wasn't allowed to eat anything with too much sugar anymore, it was his birthday week, and he was planning to indulge nonetheless.

"You look exhausted after that drive, Frankie, darling. Go and settle in the lounge and I'll bring you in a cup of tea," said Jane, fussing around the kitchen like a ball of nervous energy.

"I'd rather sit here, Mum. Then we can all go through together." After a long drive and hours to reflect on Charlie, Lilly and Robert, the last thing she wanted was to be on her own - even for another minute.

The drive down had been uneventful, and Frankie realised she could recall little about it on reflection. With the car loaded up before she settled last night, the front door had been locked, and the car was on the move by 7 am. Charlie had waved her goodbye from the field as she pulled out of the driveway. Having concocted a handful of reasonably plausible excuses, it had been possible to avoid Charlie and Lilly for the little more than 48 hours since Frankie's visit to the hospital. The idea of visiting Lilly at Charlie's house wasn't comfortable just yet. All hopes rested on seeing Robert and perhaps confirming that Charlie was simply the distraction she thought he might be. If Robert could prove to her that he could be as loving and kind as when they first met, there was every chance all thoughts of Charlie beyond friendship would melt away.

Jane placed the tea down in front of Frankie and opened a tin of biscuits. "Fancy one?"

Frankie peered into the deep tin, spotted her favourite custard creams, and grabbed a couple. "Thanks, Mum."

"Right, come on. Let's go in the other room, and you can tell us all about life in Bayscar and what you've been up to," said Martin, reaching for a biscuit and getting his hand slapped by Jane before she put the biscuit tin away on the shelf.

The day passed gently, and Frankie enjoyed being at home

again. It was nice to have people around rather than living on her own, and of course, the joy of having her meals cooked for her was indescribable! Jane asked tons of questions, and Frankie managed to answer pretty much everything. It got a bit uncomfortable when Jane tried to determine whether Charlie and Lilly had gotten together yet, and Frankie tried to say as little as possible. But Jane was like a dog with a bone, and by the time Frankie walked up the stairs towards her old bedroom, she had fully apprised Jane of Charlie and Lilly's relationship status as of three days ago and the one remaining step they may well already have taken.

Martin had left Frankie's bags in the bedroom, and as she pushed open the door, it felt like she was 15 again. Everything was pretty much as she had left it when she'd moved out into her own place; the pictures on the wall, the stickers on the tall mirror - even the bedding was the same! She sat down on the bed and stroked the duvet cover, tracing her finger over the geometric pattern like she had done so many times before. The full-length mirror was directly across from the bed, and Frankie caught sight of her reflection, expecting to see a far younger version of herself with crushing results.

The reflection that stared back looked older, for sure, but there was also a sadness in her eyes, the same sadness her mother had recognised earlier, but something Frankie hadn't noticed before. Perhaps looking in a mirror that had once reflected her young and optimistic self had highlighted the difference between then and now? Frankie didn't know why on this day, in this room and in this mirror, her sadness reflected so clearly. But there was no denying how obvious it was, and Frankie looked away.

A few minutes later, with teeth brushed and nightie on, Frankie peeled back the vintage duvet and climbed into the single bed. The mattress felt different but oh so comfortable!

She snuggled herself in and pulled the duvet up around her neck, enjoying the smell of home that erupted from the bedding as it moved.

Outside the door, Jane and Martin walked by and called to say goodnight, and then the house fell into silence. Through the open window, she could hear the faint hum of traffic, once invisible to Frankie, but after four months of living in the middle of nowhere, in total silence save the occasional owl, the noise was bothersome and hard to tune out.

Sleep wouldn't come, no matter how hard Frankie tried, and she tossed and turned, quickly losing her enthusiasm for the nostalgia of sleeping in her childhood bed. Eventually, she sat up, put the bedside light on and propped herself up with her pillows against the grey velour headboard. With just two full days before the journey back up to Bayscar on Saturday, there were a few things Frankie needed to do, the most important of which was to talk to Robert. They had spoken briefly on Monday evening and agreed that she would go to their house on Saturday morning. Their house, Frankie smiled to herself as she thought how ludicrous it felt to still own a house with Robert. She believed he would do everything to convince her to stay, but right now, only time would tell whether she would be interested in what he had to offer.

Between now and then, Frankie knew that Jane would need help with the party and keeping Martin busy while everything was set up. And Frankie wanted to spend some time alone, hoping to get her head sorted out before meeting Robert for the big talk. She had expected to spend some time in this room, but looking around in the muted lamplight, she realised that the contrast between the aspirations of teenage Frankie and everything she had become as an adult was too great. Everything about this bedroom represented failure; failure to build a career to be proud of, failure to find love and failure to start a family.

It was too much, and Frankie turned off the light again, plunging the room into darkness. As her eyes adjusted to the dark, they became heavy, and for the time being, at least, all of those feelings of failure would have to wait.

In the end, Frankie need not have concerned herself with where she would spend her spare time because thanks to the elaborate plans for Martin's surprise birthday party, there had been no spare time whatsoever! Rushing from place to place, fulfilling errand after errand, Frankie's feet had barely touched the ground. But it felt great to be out and about, doing something useful and being so busy that all of the carnage that characterised her love life was temporarily shoved into the background. Having something else to think about that didn't involve Robert, Charlie or anything to do with herself was absolute bliss, and she threw herself into every task with gusto.

The party was an enormous success, and to Jane's relief, Martin had been completely surprised when he walked into his favourite pub for a drink with his wife and daughter, to be confronted by 50 of his closest friends and family. Elizabeth's wake had taken place in the same pub, and as Frankie milled around and chatted to people, it struck her how different she felt in herself - aside from the fact she wasn't at her grandma's funeral, obviously. She felt confident and happy, enjoying people's company and not worrying about any aspect of herself or how she would be perceived. It was beyond liberating.

"Ah! There you are! I'd been hoping to catch you!" said a familiar voice as Frankie picked up a few nibbles from the buffet and arranged them on her paper plate. Unfortunately, despite a stellar effort on Frankie's part to avoid her Aunty Jean for the last two hours, the buffet was clearly a blind spot, and Jean had wasted no time making an approach.

"Hi, Aunty Jean. How are you?"

"Oh, I'm very well, dear. Very well indeed. I really can't complain about anything. I have my darling cats, and you know they bring me so much joy."

Frankie popped a sausage roll in her mouth at the exact moment Jean stopped talking, rendering her unable to do much more than nod politely.

Jean continued, undeterred by Frankie's incapacity. "And I hear things have taken a dramatic turn for you since we last saw each other—all that drama with Robert and then running off to Yorkshire with your tail between your legs. I told your dear mother; you should have tied that man down years ago. Got him to marry you while you were still young enough to be attractive and have babies."

Unable to believe what she was hearing, Frankie swallowed her food and prepared to defend herself. But Jean wasn't done.

"At your age, dear, you can't afford to be too picky or judgmental about what your man gets up to. What is it they say? Oh yes. Beggars can't be choosers. That's it. At your age, dear, the best thing to do is settle for what you can get. There can't be many fish left in the sea for you now you're in your thirties, now can there?"

There had been years of conversations like this with Jean, and Frankie had always turned the other cheek, allowing Jean to express her opinions without challenge. But this time, it was different. Frankie felt different. Enough listening; it was time to respond.

"Actually, Aunty Jean, I left to go to Yorkshire because I wanted to think about my future and whether I wanted Robert to be part of it," Frankie began, her irritation level rising by the second. "And I would rather live the rest of my life on my own than spend it in a relationship with a man that thinks so little of me that he sleeps around behind my back!"

"Ah, so that's what happened!" said Jean, delighted to have cracked open the situation to reveal the juicy nugget of gossip that Jane had so far refused to share.

Watching Jean's growing delight, Frankie's heart sank to the floor.

"…I did wonder why your mum wouldn't say. I thought to myself, it must be something like that. I mean, Robert's a good-looking man. I'm sure he gets plenty of offers, dear. I hope you thought about what you could do to hold his attention a little more while you were up there gallivanting around Yorkshire? In my experience, women should work hard to keep their men. If we stop looking after ourselves and let it all go to seed, so to speak, then, of course, the man will start to look for something prettier or more attractive."

"Thank you for your advice, Jean." Frankie dropped the 'Aunty', all inclination towards polite respect long gone. "Just out of interest, why have you lived alone, surrounded by cats, for at least 30 years?"

"Well, I…."

"And forgive me if I already knew this and have forgotten, but when were you last in a relationship? And what exactly did you do to hang on and keep them interested?"

"How dare you talk to me like that, young lady! You know very well that I chose to be single many years ago. Not that it's any of your business!" Jean started to glow a deep red, her anger bubbling up more quickly than Frankie had anticipated.

"Mum told me you were in a relationship with a guy for years, but he was married and wouldn't leave his wife for you…." Frankie wanted to carry on, but she knew she had gone too far, and Jean's eyes filled with tears.

"I don't understand why you are dragging this up and being so bloody cruel. All I wanted to do was help you. Help you avoid a life like mine. You don't want to be an old maid, living in a house full of cats because you threw your lot in with a bad apple as I did, or because you threw a decent man away through lack of care and attention. Loneliness is a cruel partner, Francesca. Now, if you don't mind, I'm going to go and talk to Deidre. I'm sure she'll be much better company."

Jean walked away, and Frankie watched as she rushed up to Deidre, said something, and then both women looked back in Frankie's direction and frowned. Frankie knew she should probably apologise, but there was still a strong feeling of resentment and anger that needed to dissipate first. Jean had no right to dole out her opinions without caring how they made people feel, especially when she didn't care too much for being on the receiving end! And plainly, she didn't.

The rest of the evening was less eventful, and Frankie enjoyed catching up with her cousins, extended family, and some very old family friends. The landlord had cleared a section of the bar to make a dance floor, and the whole place had exploded into a sea of waving arms when the DJ played 'Come on Eileen'. It was her Mum and Dad's favourite song, and for as long as Frankie could remember, every time it played, even at home, she had been dragged up to dance. Tonight, there was no dragging, though, and Frankie ran to join her parents, squeezing into position next to them on the dance floor as the first bars of the song were played.

The pub was noisy, and thanks to so many hot bodies in a small space, the air was thick and oppressive, and Frankie needed some air. So, she stepped outside into the car park and sucked in a deep breath of the fresh evening air. The gentle breeze dusted against her skin, and for a moment, she was transported back to Bayscar, where the breeze from the North Sea never stilled. But the moment was lost when her phone began to vibrate in her back pocket. She pulled it out and checked the screen, already knowing exactly what it would be and from whom. Sure enough, it was a text from Robert letting her know how much he was looking forward to seeing her tomorrow.

Frankie pushed the phone back into her pocket and looked up at the sky without sending a response. It wasn't as clear as it was in Yorkshire, she noted. The stars didn't seem as bright, and as she looked around, she realised that there was so much light all around her that it was making it harder to see the lights in the sky. The constellation of Orion was still visible but barely, and in the end, she gave up and returned her attention to the earth and the somewhat pressing issue of seeing Robert in the morning.

The altercation with Jean was unfortunate, and in some ways, Frankie felt regretful that her words had hurt Jean so much. And on reflection, Frankie began to wonder whether Jean was right on some level. Perhaps it was important to give Robert another chance, and maybe to some extent, Frankie knew that already. Throughout the four months of their separation, she had never drawn a line and said it was over; she had never fully closed the book on Robert. Sure, there had been moments where she wanted to close the book and stamp on it. But so far, she hadn't done it. The door was still open, even now.

Frankie could hear the music had slowed down inside the pub, and the night was coming to an end. The melancholic music suited her reflective mood, and she walked over to the small wall that lined the car park and sat down, being careful to take her phone from her pocket before she did so. Even a few feet from the pub doors, the music was still just audible, and Frankie recognised the song as one she had loved as a teenager. Once again, the feelings of invincibility and determination that had characterised her youth rose up and taunted the confusion and sense of personal failure that now stood in their place.

From nowhere, a mental image of Charlie popped up, and Frankie smiled as she acknowledged how much her fifteen-year-old self would have adored Charlie with his sandy blond hair, grey eyes and broad back. If Charlie had been a pop star back in the day, he would have been plastered all over teenage Frankie's bedroom walls for sure!

The pub doors opened, and Dylan, Frankie's youngest cousin, now 19, ran out in the opposite direction to where Frankie was sitting and promptly threw up.

"Sorry!" he called across to Frankie as he ambled back into the pub, wiping his mouth on his shirt sleeve as he went.

"I'm no teenager…. thank God," said Frankie to the empty car park.

And heaven knows, Charlie was no pop star. As Frankie strolled towards the pub, she resolved to talk to Robert in the morning with an open mind, listen to what he wanted to say and take things from there. Finally, she could see that the future was hers to determine, though, and as long as it didn't involve a houseful of cats and a penchant for gossip, whatever happened next was just fine.

Chapter 17

The silence was deafening as Frankie readied herself not only for leaving her parents but also for the ordeal of the conversation she was about to have with Robert. She sipped a large mug of coffee, gazing out of the window, listening to the inane babble on the radio and missing concerned glances from both Martin and Jane.

Finally, she pulled herself off the stool and away from the breakfast bar, walking towards the hallway where the sight of her packed bags made her feel a little sad. The family shared farewells with hugs and tears.

"Just do what's right for you, Frankie, no-one else, just you," Martin whispered as Frankie walked through the front door.

"Thanks, Dad. I love you both so much."

Frankie turned away, so they didn't see her tears; she couldn't see their tears either as they waved goodbye.

Across town, and feeling like he was a teenager on his first date, Robert buzzed around the house, straightening cushions, moving the vase of flowers on the coffee table by half an inch to the right and checking his appearance in the hall mirror for the umpteenth time. Frankie was minutes away, and everything needed to be so perfect that she would never want to leave him again. The loneliness and misery of the past few months had surprised Robert, and he knew that he didn't want to experience it again. But, if the next few hours went well, he felt sure she would stay. He felt ready for the commitment Frankie had always craved.

Robert checked the coffee had brewed and lit the scented candles he had dotted around the lounge and kitchen to give the house a welcoming feeling. As he checked himself in the mirror one more time, he heard a car pull onto the driveway, and sure enough, Frankie's car was exactly where it should always have been - next to his.

Frankie stood on the doorstep, unsure whether to knock or let herself in, but it didn't matter in the end because Robert opened the door and beamed at her.

"You're here!" he gushed, standing aside so Frankie could walk into her own home.

"I am indeed," she replied, marvelling at how infantile their first words were and hoping things improved quickly.

The house smelled lovely, and she spotted one of her candles on the sideboard in the hallway. As she moved into the lounge, more candles flickered in their glass holders on the mantlepiece, the windowsill and next to the TV. The room was tidy and clean, and even the cushions looked plumped and perfectly aligned with each other. Frankie smiled, touched at the effort Robert had clearly made for her visit.

She pulled off her jacket, and before she could even think about where to put it, Robert was there to take it from her.

"Let me," he said simply. "Go through to the kitchen. Breakfast is ready."

Frankie walked into the kitchen and remembered her final morning, lying on the settee over to the left, watching the rainfall and trying to work out what to do. As she stood looking at the pastries and fresh fruit on the breakfast bar, smelled the freshly brewed coffee and noted the enormous bouquet waiting on what she presumed to be her seat, she felt a million miles from that damp and miserable morning in January.

"I hope you are okay with pastries? I wasn't sure what you wanted, so I thought this was safest. But I have some smoked salmon in the fridge if you prefer? I could make some eggs?"

Frankie could tell Robert was nervous, and she felt terrible for him. "This is fine, Robert. Honestly, it's lovely."

Robert seemed to relax slightly, and Frankie felt bad that he was in such a state. Robert was never nervous, and this was a side to him she hadn't seen since they first met. Back then, he had tried hard to make a good impression; they both had.

Frankie walked over to the big glass doors and looked out at the garden. It was well kept, and her rose bushes were beginning to flower. She noticed that Robert had even tied one of the bushes to a cane to stop it from breaking under the weight of its buds. And he had put some food in her bird feeder too. Every small revelation chipped away at the shield she had placed around her heart.

"Shall we eat?" he asked, and as Frankie turned, he held out the bouquet of deep pink peonies, and Frankie accepted them. They were exquisite.

"Thank you so much, Robert. They are so beautiful!"

"As are you," he replied quietly - so quietly in fact, that Frankie was unsure she'd heard him correctly.

Before she could figure out whether to ask him what he'd said, he turned and pulled out Frankie's seat. She placed the peonies on the small table next to the settee and walked over to take her seat. Once she was comfortable, Robert sat down too.

Still nervous, Robert hopped on and off his stool, getting things from the fridge, grabbing some kitchen roll when he spilt some coffee as he poured it from the jug, and in the end, Frankie couldn't take it anymore.

"Robert! Please relax! You are like a cat on a hot tin roof! Honestly, this is all lovely. The house looks lovely. You've gone to so much trouble, and it is all fine. It's better than fine. It's perfect! So please, just relax now, okay? It's only me...."

Frankie meant every word. He had made such a considerable effort; it was mind-blowing. And it hadn't escaped her notice that this breakfast was the one thing she had most wanted to do when she moved into the house all those years ago; a lazy breakfast on Saturday morning, just the two of them, looking out over the garden enjoying their beautiful home. The familiarity of the surroundings felt terrific, and Frankie felt herself begin to relax. She just hoped Robert could settle too.

"Frankie, I know we have a lot to talk about, but for now, I want you to know it is wonderful to have you here." Robert stopped there, determined to avoid his emotions getting the better of him. He grabbed his coffee and took a swig, immediately regretting his decision.

"Are you okay?" Frankie asked as Robert put his coffee down and wrinkled his nose in pain.

"I burned my tongue on the coffee!" he cried, reaching for a glass of water.

Frankie battled against the memory of Charlie burning his tongue in the hospital cafe just days ago but was powerless to stop her mind from filling with the image of Charlie, barely breaking a sweat, sitting quietly and holding her gaze. She shivered, and Robert noticed.

"Are you cold?"

"No, I'm fine. Sorry. How's your mouth now?" Frankie asked, making herself focus on her breakfast and clearing her mind of everything.

"Oh, it's fine. I'll probably have a blister, but it'll be okay. You take care, though - the coffee is hot."

Once breakfast was finished, and everything was tidied away, they moved into the lounge and sat down next to each other on the large black leather sofa that Frankie had always hated, but Robert refused to replace. The symbolism of the furniture wasn't lost on Robert either, and he quickly announced that he wanted to get rid of the leather furniture and buy something that suited them both. Frankie was grateful and said as much, the scale of change that Robert seemed prepared to make to bring Frankie back into his life becoming more apparent by the hour. Every gesture softened Frankie slightly, and she could feel herself becoming comfortable again. But not entirely.

"Mum said one of her friends saw you in town with another woman a couple of months ago. Have you been seeing anyone while I've been away?"

Robert looked down and considered his response. "You know I was seeing someone when you left because that's why you wanted to go. When you left, I was angry. Really angry, actually, and I didn't stop seeing Audrey for a few weeks. I'm not proud of it, and I'm deeply sorry. But, Frankie, I was so angry and hurt. It wasn't a good decision and as soon as I realised that, I finished it. And it was over long before I came up to see you."

It was Frankie's turn to look at the floor as she tried to figure out how she felt about what Robert had just said. She had to concede it was honest. He wasn't lying to her, and that was a step forward. And he was sorry and regretful, and that was a huge step forward. The cogs in her mind turned furiously, trying to figure out what this meant to her.

"Did she ever sleep here?" Even Frankie was surprised when that question popped out!

"No. Never. I would never do that, Frank. Never."

The answer was categoric, and Frankie believed him. "Okay."

They sat in silence for a few minutes, trying to figure out how to begin the conversation again. In the end, it was Robert who took the plunge.

"While we're on the subject of apologies, I also want to say how sorry I am again for the scene I caused when I came up to see you. The way I behaved with Charlie....it was unforgivable. I felt ashamed afterwards. I hope you can forgive me?"

"I wouldn't be here if I hadn't forgiven you, Robert."

"I was just so jealous of your life up there, and if I'm honest..." the truth came tumbling out of Robert like a waterfall after weeks of anticipation. "...I was jealous of him. Of Charlie. I could see you were friends, and he was so bloody tall and fit looking. I felt short and flabby. He made me feel inadequate, Frank. The thought of you being up there with him - and I know there was nothing between you - it just made me feel sick."

Frankie watched as the man she had known and loved for seven years turned himself inside out in front of her eyes. He was almost in tears, pouring out his truth and laying it bare to win her back. It was overwhelming and so touching. Robert was so different.

"Charlie is with Lilly," Frankie whispered.

"What?"

"Charlie and Lilly are together now. Just this last weekend, in fact."

To his shame, Robert felt a wave of relief, and Frankie could see it written large across his face. She knew that sharing the news of Charlie and Lilly would put Robert's mind at rest. It was a neat and tidy ending to a situation that would otherwise have been complicated for both Frankie and Robert.

"How do you feel about that?" Robert asked before realising how it sounded. He hastily continued, "I mean, does that make it a bit awkward for you as you are all friends? Like the three of you? Three is an awkward number...." He knew he was rambling, so he stopped.

"I'm fine with it. I've known that they like each other for a while, so it was just a matter of them figuring it out." The thought of Charlie and Lilly flashed through Frankie's mind, and she batted it away. She wasn't as okay with it as she wanted to be…. yet.

"Do you fancy going for a walk?" Robert asked, changing the subject to their mutual relief.

They pulled the front door closed five minutes later and set off to explore the local park.

Frankie hadn't ever explored the area on foot. She had embraced walking with a passion since moving up north, but around here, in the suburbs, it had never occurred to her to venture out and see a bit more of where she lived. It was grim to begin with, picking their way through the housing estate and past a large industrial unit with loading bays and huge artic lorries lined up to be filled with goodness knows what. As she walked, she wondered what Charlie would make of where she lived, and she smiled to herself at the face he would probably pull.

Eventually, they found a large park lined with trees, and Frankie began to enjoy the experience a little more. There was a junior football league running a tournament at one end, and a cluster of parents stood at the side of each of the three pitches, cheering on their children as they raced around the field.

Frankie stopped to watch, and Robert watched Frankie. He knew she had longed for a family, and he had stood between her and that dream for years. It was just one of a million things he regretted, but unlike many of the self-serving decisions he had made that were irretrievable, this was something he could address.

"Do you still want children, Frank?" he asked softly as she watched a small boy run towards her to collect a rogue ball.

Frankie was surprised by the question and answered instinctively, not anticipating what would follow. "Yes, very much."

Robert closed his eyes and took a breath. This was a huge step to take, but by God, he was ready to take it. "I would love for us to start a family."

Frankie's head snapped around to face him, her attention now entirely on what Robert had just said. "What?"

"I said, I would love for us to start a family together."

"Are you serious? Do you mean this, Robert? Don't play with me?"

Robert smiled and took Frankie's hand in his own. "I'm not playing with you. No more games, Frank. I mean it. Let's start a family."

Frankie felt a sudden rush of joy and lost herself in the moment, throwing her arms around Robert's neck and hugging him for the first time in months. They both laughed, and as she pulled away again, Robert wanted to kiss her, but he held back. He knew this couldn't be rushed. Everything had to be at Frankie's pace if this was going to work.

They continued to walk, and Frankie's mind was buzzing with the possibility of being a mum and having her own family. It was the most incredible prospect, and one she had never imagined would result from seeing Robert today.

The conversation flowed nicely, and they talked about many things, including places they would both like to go on holiday. Robert cautiously planted a seed in Frankie's mind about maybe going somewhere in the Caribbean towards the end of the year, and she accepted the idea. Everything they discussed was kept loose and hypothetical, but beneath the surface, plans were developing, a life together was beginning to take shape by stealth.

Frankie was having a good time as they walked along, and she couldn't believe how relaxed she felt in Robert's company or how different Robert seemed to be. He was like a new man. A new and improved version of Robert Hughes. And it was all very wonderful. But in the midst of all the wonderful was the niggling feeling of being in the wrong place. The person might be right, but the scenery was wrong. The walk was pleasant enough, but there was no way a suburban park surrounded by thousands of houses and industrial warehouses could eclipse or even match the beauty of the North Yorkshire coastline. If she were to build a life with Robert - and she was more open to it than ever - she would lose her connection to the sea, the cliffs and the peace and tranquillity of the village. And she'd miss Charlie's farm and all the animals.

The universe evidently wanted to hammer the point home because an eruption of sirens shattered the relative quiet of their walk as four police cars and two ambulances shot down the main road that ran behind the housing estate.

"Would we have to live here?" Frankie asked, without thinking, leaving Robert with a sizeable dilemma he knew he couldn't avoid.

"Would you want to live in Bayscar?" he replied, hoping upon hope he could manage this and get the result he needed.

"I do love it there. So yes, I suppose I would like to. But I know it's a bit remote...." She trailed off, knowing there was little chance Robert would agree, making any further effort pretty futile.

"I would struggle to find work anywhere close by. And the cottage won't be suitable for a growing family." Robert paused, quietly pleased with how clever that last point was. "But we could keep the cottage as a holiday home if you like?

Maybe look to extend it, so it has another bedroom? We'd need three bedrooms if we have a couple of kids...."

Frankie felt torn. Her love for the cottage, the village and the coastline it sat on was beyond even her understanding, but the thought of having a family..... It was simply a dream come true. Robert had suggested a compromise, and as long as she could spend plenty of time up there each year, she felt sure she could make it work. And Charlie could keep an eye on the cottage. She felt sure he would do that for her.

She nodded, and they held hands as they walked back into their street and towards their house.

Robert made them both a cup of coffee, and they settled down again in the lounge. Time was pressing, and Frankie needed to get going if she wanted to be back in Bayscar before darkness fell. Although she was getting better at driving between the motorway and the village, the network of narrow lanes would be much more frightening to navigate in the dark, and it wasn't something she was ready to attempt.

"So, what's it going to be then, Frank?" Robert asked. "Are we going to make a go of this? Of us?"

Frankie blew on her coffee as the steam rose, and she carefully weighed up the question. There was no doubt Robert had changed. And he had offered the life she had always wanted to have with him. She felt comfortable around him, and they had enjoyed a lovely morning together. And then, of course, there was the possibility of becoming a mother. It was all so much more than she had expected.

Robert was on edge, waiting for Frankie to answer, and he pulled off his signet ring and began to roll it between his fingers absentmindedly. Frankie couldn't take her eyes off the ring, and her mind filled with the memory of Charlie rolling his wedding ring in the same way.

Charlie. Always Charlie. Every thought, every moment seems to be linked to Charlie, Frankie thought to herself.

She closed her eyes, trying to push him from her mind.

"Frankie?" Robert pressed.

When she opened her eyes, the ring was back on his finger, and she felt a wave of relief.

"Sorry, Robert. I…" She didn't know what to say, how to frame how she felt. How did she feel? So much hope and possibility existed here, in this house. "I've had such a wonderful morning. We've had such a lovely time together. I think…."

Robert's face was alive with hope, and Frankie knew she held his heart in the palm of her hand.

"…I think we should give it a try," she said finally.

Robert leapt to his feet, and Frankie did the same. They came together in the middle of the room and wrapped their arms around each other, their bodies pressed against each other. Robert placed a tender kiss on Frankie's forehead, still cautious not to push her too far too quickly, setting aside his desperate need to lose himself in her hair, in her body, in every inch of her.

He pulled Frankie tightly to his chest and held her close, and she rested her head against him, his arms wrapped around her. She listened as his heart beat quickly in his chest and felt the warmth of his body through his clothes. She closed her eyes and tried to fight the overwhelming urge to compare with all her might. But it was impossible. There was no way to ignore the memory of Charlie, of Charlie's arms holding her against *his* body, of Charlie's heart beating so hard in *his* chest. Charlie, Charlie, Charlie.

Suddenly Lilly's words came flooding back - *and if it feels even the slightest bit wrong, you haul ass and get back up here where you belong* - and it did feel wrong. But not because Robert wasn't trying, wasn't loving, wasn't changed. It was because Frankie had changed. Yorkshire had changed her, and the life she had up there was the life she wanted, with or without Charlie.

"I can't do this!" she cried, pulling away from Robert without warning.

"What's going on? I thought...." Robert was confused. Everything he had worked so hard for was suddenly slipping through his fingers. "Frank? I thought we were going to be together?"

Frankie's mind raced as she stood, frozen to the spot, without any clue what she was doing. Robert was staring at her, his utter confusion wrestling with growing frustration, and yet, face to face with Robert and the awkward atmosphere she had created, all she could do was think about Charlie.

"I need to go. I'm sorry, Robert. I can't do this. I can't be... this," she said, gathering up her bag and jacket from the hallway.

"Is this about Charlie?" Robert asked as she moved towards the door. "You love him, don't you?"

And then the strangest thing happened. Frankie knew precisely what she felt and what she needed to say.

"It is about Charlie, yes. But I am not leaving this house and walking away from you because I want to be with Charlie. Charlie is with Lilly, and I respect and support that completely. This is about Charlie because all morning, every single thing I have thought about, I have seen through Charlie's eyes, I have wondered what Charlie would think or what Charlie would say. And do you know what that tells me?"

Robert shook his head, unable to take in what was unfolding in his hallway.

"It tells me that I don't love you enough, Robert. It tells me that no matter how much you change or how wonderful a life you promise to give me, I cannot give you all of myself. I can't offer you every piece of who I am because I think about him. All the time. I have to work through that, and I will."

"But we could work through it together? You said yourself you can't be with Charlie so why not stay here and see whether we can make this work? You can forget about him, and I can help you. We could do this together. We don't have to be apart. I'm prepared to wait for you, Frank...."

"Robert, darling, Robert, I know you want this to work and I'm so grateful that you have made such an effort for me. Honestly, I am. But I don't want to be here, living in this street, in this town, in the middle of the country with no sea within a hundred bloody miles! I want to be up there, with my friends, on my cliff and in my cottage."

"I'll move up there with you. I'll give up my job. We can sell the house!"

"No, Robert. Your life is here. You're a good man, and you deserve someone who wants to live the same life you want. It's not me anymore. Maybe it was never me. Let me go, please."

"What if he never leaves her, Frank? What if he stays with Lilly, and you have to watch them be together forever? How will you be able to stomach that? Life doesn't have to be that hard for you Frankie. You don't need to be there to watch them create a life that you aren't part of."

"Robert, if you knew Charlie and Lilly, you would know they will always be together. They are made for each other. They need each other. But what I now understand more clearly than ever is that I need them. As my friends. I want them to be happy, and I know that for me to be happy, I need to be up there with them. I need to be in Bayscar. That's the life I want."

"Then go, Frank. Just go." Robert looked like he had lost everything, and it broke Frankie's heart to see him that way.

But she wasn't going to change her mind.

"I'm sorry, Robert. I really am."

Robert looked down for a moment and considered his response. He knew he had lost her, the bright light in her eyes reflecting the renewed spirit that being in Yorkshire had ignited in her. Treating her so badly and then letting her go had been the single biggest mistake of his life and there was no denying that all he wanted in the world was to beg her to stay.

"No, I'm sorry, Frankie. I was careless, and I didn't pay attention. I lost you. I let you go. So, go. And be happy."

Chapter 18

As Frankie closed the door on what had been her home for the last seven years or so, with a promise that Robert would send on her possessions in due course, she knew that she was closing the door on her past life. Her relationship with Robert was finally at an end. All the hopes and fears, regrets, and false promises were behind her, and the decision to make her home in the North Yorkshire village she had come to love so much was entirely hers. Frankie felt in charge of her own destiny for the first time in years. She felt relieved and proud of the person she had become over the past few months. As she opened the car door, she realised that the cliché was true, for her at least; this really was the beginning of the rest of her life.

"Time to go," she said aloud, looking back at the house one last time. But first, there was one thing she needed to do. She didn't want to send her parents a quick text or call them with her news, so she drove to their house, parked the car outside on the road, and rang the bell.

"Frankie, love. What are you doing back here?" asked Jane with surprise as she opened the door.

"It's done. I've left Robert for good. My home is in Bayscar now." But, seeing the sadness in her mum's eyes, she added, "It's where I belong, Mum. I am so happy there. I can see that now."

"I know. You're just like your grandma, my darling, and she would be so very, very proud of you right now."

They both went to find Martin in the garden. Frankie explained the entire situation to them both, eliciting surprise from Jane as she explained how influential Charlie had been in the decision, despite his relationship with Lilly.

"Well, I had no idea you liked him, dear. But I can certainly see why you would! Will you be able to stand seeing him with Lilly?"

"Mum, I'll be fine about it. They are great together, and they both deserve to be happy. There's enough joy for me in just being around them both and living on the coast."

"Well, you know your own mind, Francesca, that's for sure. We are in awe of you for having the courage to go up there and strike out on your own. Whatever you think is right for you is okay by us," said Martin, trowel in hand and hands covered in mud.

With time pressing on, Frankie wrenched herself away and back to the car, sadness mixed with excitement as she waved her parents goodbye.

The journey back to Bayscar was a dream; the roads and motorway were all free-flowing, and there were no hold-ups or road works to impede Frankie's journey. In fact, with the sun shining, her sunglasses on, and music blaring from the stereo, the three hours in the car had been a surprisingly enjoyable experience.

There was no way of ignoring the change in how she felt compared to the last time she had taken the same path. On that dreary day in January, her heart smashed into pieces, and with no clear idea what she wanted from her future, Frankie had practically limped into Yorkshire, a broken and hopeless figure, buried in grief for the loss of her relationship. On that miserable day, the skies had been grey and menacing, the traffic had been hideous, and there was no singing along to upbeat music. Put simply, on 17th January, there had been no joy.

The scenery to the sides of the motorway started to change, and the endless level fields became undulating hills and even the motorway itself seemed to incline slightly as though the car were climbing up the country. Eventually, Frankie reached the exit that would take her off towards the east coast, and as she circled the roundabout and pulled onto the road that would lead her in the direction of the sea, her heart swelled.

And Frankie wasn't the only person heading in the direction of the stunning Yorkshire coastline. Cars pulling caravans of varying sizes peppered the road. But, although they slowed her progress, as she waited for the chance to overtake or followed them slowly to where they would turn off, nothing could diminish Frankie's sense of optimism and contentment.

Walking away from Robert and her home just a few hours earlier was unexpected. As she drove, she reflected on how excited she had been about the idea of starting a family and the plans she and Robert had begun to make. By the time they were enjoying what would be their final coffee together, the decision to rebuild their relationship was pretty much made. Robert had only asked out of courtesy, their previous conversations about starting a family more than implying a future together. And when she stood up and accepted that future, in many ways, she had meant it.

But her life in Bayscar was too important, and she had needed Charlie to guide her to that conclusion. That's why she had thought about him so often when she was with Robert. Charlie was an integral part of everything she loved about Bayscar, but in the same way, she didn't love Robert enough because she was attracted to Charlie; she couldn't possibly love Charlie if she was considering life - and children - with Robert. Both men had served a purpose, guiding her to a new life by the sea.

She didn't want Charlie. All she wanted was for Charlie and Lilly to be happy together. The most important thing about returning to Bayscar was that it represented a choice, a firm decision that she had made about her future, without any romantic obligation or complication. She wanted to live by the sea and be surrounded by the community in Bayscar. She wanted to work at the hotel and build a life based on hard work and satisfaction. She was staying in North Yorkshire.

As she drove into the village, everything looked the same. The hotel was a hive of activity. The tea shop was busy with people sitting outside on the tiny terrace Rose had created to the side of the building. The path that led down towards the golf course and the cliff edge was dotted with couples and families, excited children running around and dogs straining at their leashes, keen to run free in the long seagrasses up ahead. The sight of the North Sea brought a joyful smile to Frankie's face, the sun sparkling across its surface like a blanket of diamonds. She would never tire of that view.

Slowing to turn onto the track and towards the cottage, Frankie saw Tash, her husband and children walking in the direction of the small parade of shops. Tash waved, and Frankie smiled and waved back. There was no doubt in her mind that she was a part of this community now. She was home.

Approaching her own cottage, Frankie decided she would go straight down to Charlie's farmhouse and see how Lilly was doing. Having avoided them both before she went to Buckinghamshire, it was time to face them again, celebrate their union and enjoy being in their company once more.

Charlie would never know the full extent of his influence on Frankie's decision to come back here and build her future in Yorkshire, and it was undoubtedly better that way for them both. But it was essential to Frankie that she found as many ways to thank him as she could, and embracing his love for Lilly was the least she could do.

Continuing down the track, the farmhouse came into sight, but there was no sign of Charlie's truck in his driveway. Instead, his usual parking space was filled with a small yellow hatchback that Frankie didn't recognise. She knew it wasn't Lilly's car, which was probably parked in its designated space behind her flat. The hatchback was a distinctive colour, and Frankie thought she might have seen it before, but she couldn't place it and quickly dismissed it as unimportant.

She pulled up alongside the mystery vehicle and stepped out into the fresh coastal breeze, drawing in a deep breath, filling her lungs with the clear, refreshing air she had missed so much, even after such a short absence.

Grabbing her bag, she locked the car and walked towards the front door, which was slightly open. There was no sign of the dogs, and Frankie wondered if perhaps they were out in the fields. But Lilly should be inside. She eased the door open slightly and called out, but there was no answer.

Unsure what to do and wondering if the door was even meant to be open, Frankie peered inside and shouted again. There was still no response, but she caught the faint sound of someone laughing from somewhere inside. It was a woman's laugh and so assuming it was Lilly, Frankie opened the door and walked in.

"Hello?" she called, and once again, no one responded.

Another burst of laughter came from the kitchen, so Frankie walked straight ahead and opened the kitchen door. Then, as her eyes adjusted to the kitchen's brightness after the relative darkness of the hallway, she took in the scene at the far side of the room and clamped her hand over her mouth. She'd happened upon something she couldn't make sense of - Lilly in the arms of someone who wasn't Charlie. Frankie was appalled and, unnoticed, turned to leave as quietly as she could. But in her haste to escape, she banged her foot into a stool which fell to the tiled floor. Lilly looked up and spotted a retreating Frankie, but it was too late. Frankie bolted from the house and into the afternoon sunshine, her whole body shaking with confusion and shock.

"Frankie, wait!" cried Lilly, tugging her top down with her one good hand as she ran outside.

"I'm sorry, I shouldn't have come in!" Frankie replied, fumbling in her bag for her car keys.

"Frankie, please. Stop a minute. Talk to me. I can explain...."

Frankie's head was spinning, and her blood was racing through her veins. She felt disoriented and lost, all of the joy and contentment she had bathed in as she drove down the track now ripped from her and replaced by abject confusion. She had been so convinced that Lilly and Charlie were solid together, that their relationship was based on trust and love - she had said as much to Robert just hours ago! Frankie could never have anticipated this – that Lilly was actually involved with someone else.

Unable to look at Lilly, she kicked at a small stone and stared at the dusty driveway. It was all just a distraction, and Lilly was determinedly not going anywhere, leaving Frankie with no choice but to face whatever Lilly wanted to say.

"Frankie?" Lilly pressed.

Frankie looked up and met her eyes. The first thing she saw was fear, which made sense. But she also saw pride, and that confused matters even more.

"Go on then...."

"What did you see?" Lilly asked, unsure where to start and reasoning a quick fact check was as good a place as any.

Frankie raised an eyebrow at the question but answered it anyway. "I saw you and whoever that was…." She waved her hands in the direction of the front door. "…in the middle of something pretty intimate." There was an angry note in her voice, and she couldn't help it. How dare Lilly be unfaithful to Charlie when their relationship was only days old!

"Right…" Lilly trailed off, trying to figure out what to say next, but Frankie wasn't finished.

"The thing is, Lilly. I know that you and Charlie are together. Perhaps not together yet, but you are clearly going to be together. I mean, it's obvious he loves you, and I thought it was obvious that you love him, at least until this happened. How could you do this to Charlie? How could you do something to hurt him so badly when he's been through so much already!"

Lilly burst out laughing from nowhere, and it stopped Frankie in her tracks.

"How can you find this funny?" Frankie cried, her anger at Lilly's attitude to hurting Charlie growing by the second.

"Because it *is* funny!" cried Lilly between waves of mirth. "Me and Charlie! That's hilarious!"

Frankie stood silently and watched as Lilly laughed so hard, she had tears streaming down her cheeks. She bent double, holding her tummy with her good arm, her bad arm hanging in its sling, redundant. No one else was around, and whoever was in the cottage hadn't yet shown their face. Frankie wondered who it could be.

Eventually, Lilly stopped laughing and gathered herself together. "I think we need to talk. Come and sit with me." Lilly steered Frankie over to a wooden bench on the far side of the driveway, giving a clear view across the fields to the sea beyond.

"Charlie said Katie used to enjoy sitting here before she got too ill," said Lilly quietly. "She loved the sea, apparently." She had a distant look, and Frankie wondered what on earth was going on in Lilly's mind. So much didn't make sense.

"Lilly, who was that in there?" Frankie asked quietly, keeping her eyes focussed on the view.

"Annabel," said Lilly, her voice barely a whisper.

"Annabel, the bridesmaid?"

"Annabel, my girlfriend, who I got together with when she was a bridesmaid."

"Your girlfriend?" Frankie was aghast. How did she not know?

"Yep. I'm gay."

The two women sat in silence for a moment or two as the dust settled on Lilly's revelation. For Lilly, the relief at having told Frankie her biggest secret was immense. Sharing her sexuality with anyone was excruciatingly hard, especially given that she'd experienced so much anger at home when her parents had inadvertently found out. It had taken a while before she had felt able to confide in Charlie, and since then, she had told only Sue and Pete.

"I had no idea," Frankie said, turning to face her friend.

"I have wanted to tell you so badly, Frank. From the day I met you, I wanted you to know. But I was just so scared of what you'd say...."

"Lilly, I love you. You are my friend. I don't care whether you are straight or gay. You are Lilly Sunday. My friend Lilly. Nothing changes that. Nothing." Frankie's eyes filled with tears, a whisper of sadness that her friend hadn't felt able to share who she truly was.

"And you're my friend, Frankie. But I needed to be sure. Charlie said you'd be fine with it, but how could I just come out and say it after we spent so many hours talking about who we were, what had brought us to Bayscar. And I never told you then, at the beginning. I left it too long, and then it was impossible. I should have been braver. I wish I had been braver and just told you straight away...."

They embraced and held each other, one crying their tears onto the other's shoulder, neither willing to let go and break the precious shared moment of love and understanding. But the impracticality of an arm in a sling and the inflexibility of a wooden bench meant the embrace was short-lived, the two women easing apart and stretching their backs out slightly.

"What did happen in Harrogate, Lilly?" Frankie asked, hopeful that she would be able to piece Lilly's life together at last.

"My parents are pretty religious. Dad's from Nigeria and Mum's Irish, and they're both pretty traditional, old-fashioned types, you know? So, they wanted me to settle down and marry a nice Catholic boy, and for a long time, I was too scared to tell them I didn't want that. I tried telling them I was a modern woman; I should be able to make my own choices, that kind of thing. I introduced them to some of my gay friends, and they were very welcoming and accepting over time; I started to think that maybe it would be okay if I came out to them. But they found out in an awful way. One of my cousins saw me with a girl and told my aunt, who told my mum. It turned into this big family scandal, and in the end, it wasn't even about me being gay. It was about the fact I hadn't told them. It was messed up! I had to leave. Even now, more than two years later, there are still people in the family that won't talk to me. Mum and Dad are great about it now, but there's too much blame and hate in my family. So, I stay away."

Frankie placed her arm around Lilly's shoulders and pulled her in for a gentle hug, careful not to hurt her bad arm.

"I'm so sorry, Lilly. I really am." Frankie was devastated that her friend had gone through so much and felt privileged that Lilly had finally shared the truth with her.

"What about Charlie?" Frankie asked, aware she was shifting the focus away from Lilly's past but unable to ignore the mystery of his role in the situation.

"Charlie's known I'm gay for almost two years. He's been like a brother to me, helping me come to terms with what happened in Harrogate...."

"I thought you were together...." Frankie admitted, somewhat unnecessarily. Her reaction to Lilly's 'infidelity' something of a clue to her assumptions.

"Me and Charlie! God, no!" Lilly laughed. "I can't believe you ever thought we were a thing! Why on earth did you think that?"

"Well, you spend all your time together; you are always hugging and ruffling his hair. Even my mum thought you were a couple!" Frankie felt foolish as she spoke.

"Your mum! I thought she was a bit savvier than that! I'm disappointed!" laughed Lilly with a mischievous grin.

"And then, at the hospital...." Frankie began but then stopped, figuring out the best way to say what she wanted. "At the hospital, Charlie talked about being ready to stop wearing his ring. He was definitely implying he was ready for some kind of relationship. So, I guessed it must be you." As she wound up speaking, she knew it sounded sketchy. There were so many assumptions in her theory, so much guessing. She began to doubt her own logic.

On one side of the bench, Lilly stayed quiet for a moment and considered what she should say. Frankie wasn't so far off the mark, but Charlie was a very private man, and Lilly didn't want to break his confidence. He had held her secret for so long there was no way she could ever do anything to hurt him. Charlie was the closest thing to a brother Lilly had. After her parents, Charlie was the closest family she had, full stop.

From her side of the bench, Frankie watched as her friend wrestled with something, but unclear what. Perhaps telling Lilly about Charlie and his ring had made Lilly realise Charlie was in love with her. Just because you know someone is gay doesn't mean you can't fall in love with them, she reasoned.

The silence extended beyond the point of comfort, and both women shifted slightly in their seats, fighting the urge to share their thoughts and breathe life back into the conversation. Both believed they held a perspective that needed to be shared but lacked the confidence to share it, fearing the implications for their friendships with each other and with Charlie if they did.

In the end, it was Lilly who spoke first.

Chapter 19

"It's you," said Lilly simply, not shifting her focus from the sun as it dipped lower in the sky, rays of light piercing through the gathering clouds.

"What did you say?" Frankie asked, unsure she had heard Lilly correctly.

"I said, it's you, Frank. Charlie's in love with you."

Adrenalin shot through Frankie's entire body, every limb, every organ, tingling with a mixture of terror and excitement. Her heart began to race, and a million thoughts and questions tore through her mind.

"How do you know?"

Lilly turned to face Frankie and smiled at her starstruck expression, the perfect blend of shock and delight. "What, you mean apart from the fact he is totally soppy every time he's around you? Or the fact that he would do anything for you?"

Frankie's excitement dimmed just a fraction. "He does anything for everyone, Lilly. Not just me. And he's not soppy around me. I can't imagine Charlie being soppy!"

"Trust me, Frank. He's daft about you."

Frankie didn't believe it. Nothing Lilly had said was any more reliable than Frankie's conclusions about Charlie's feelings for Lilly, just more assumptions and guessing. "It's all nonsense, Lilly. He's no more in love with me than he is with you. We've both got the wrong end of the stick."

Lilly watched as her friend mentally boxed away all of the excitement and hope that had risen at the suggestion Charlie was in love with her. The starstruck look was carefully packed away to be replaced by a slight frown, and Lilly knew Frankie well enough to know that the next thing shee would do would be to get up and try to leave.

"Right, I'd better head back to the cottage. It's been a long day," said Frankie on cue, causing Lilly to laugh again.

"What's so funny?" Frankie asked, standing up and brushing the back of her jeans as her irritation increased. All she wanted to do was go home. After the long drive and all of the confusion about Lilly and Annabel, she needed to be on her own and maybe even take a long hot bubble bath with a large glass of wine.

"Frankie, sit back down...."

"No, I'm going...." Frankie began to walk away, and Lilly stood up.

"He told me he's in love with you." Lilly winced as she spoke, knowing that she hadn't just broken Charlie's confidence with that single statement; she had smashed it into tiny pieces.

Without a word, Frankie walked back to the bench and sat down, staring straight ahead across the fields, her face a picture of shock. "He did?"

"He did. But he also thinks that right now, you are down south, making sweet love to that grim little man you seem unable to leave, and Charlie thinks you still love." Lilly wrinkled her nose in disgust at the thought of Robert, having been wholly unable to fathom what it was that Frankie found appealing in such an unimpressive little man.

The concept of making love to Robert was so unappealing to Frankie that she burst out laughing, although triggered by relief rather than amusement. She had come so close to committing her entire life to Robert just hours ago, and surely by now, if she had stayed, they would have made love. The thought horrified her, and the laughing continued.

Lilly watched as her friend worked through her feelings, and even though Frankie was smiling and laughing, it was impossible to miss the tears that were threatening to fall as she wrestled with how close she had come to a future she could no longer face.

"I've told Robert it's over. I'm back up here to stay. I left him this morning…." Frankie managed, calming at last. The reality of what lay ahead with Charlie was beginning to sink in, and that made her feel nervous, cutting off the laughter in a heartbeat.

"Well, in that case, I suggest you get in your car, drive back up that track and go tell Charlie, because for pretty much all of the last three days, he's been at your cottage, fixing up your decking so you can sell the place when you go back to Robert. Lovesick fool!" Lilly smiled at Frankie as she spoke, watching as the hope flared in her friend's eyes. "Well, go on! What are you waiting for?"

Frankie leapt up, hugged Lilly, and ran to her car. She had no idea what she would say when she got there, but all she wanted to do was get back to the cottage and see Charlie. The rest would just have to work itself out.

However, Charlie's truck wasn't there when she pulled up outside the cottage. Still, Frankie rushed into the back garden to ensure he wasn't there, casting aside every shred of logic in her quest to find him. But there was no sign of him, just a stunning new deck to replace the death trap that had been there just days before. She vowed to check it out properly when she had tracked Charlie down and hurried back to the road. Deciding there was no time to go into the cottage and that it would be wiser to go on foot, so when she found

Charlie, they only had one vehicle to deal with, she set off up the hill towards the hotel, rechecking her phone in case anyone - Charlie - had made contact.

As she passed the tearoom, Rose came outside to clear some tables. "Hello dear! You're back! How wonderful. How was your dad's party?"

"It went well, thanks, Rose. He enjoyed the fuss we made of him. Have you seen Charlie by any chance?" she asked hopefully. Not much happened in Bayscar without Rose knowing about it.

"Not for a few hours, dear. He popped in this morning and was no more cheerful than he's been all week. Bless him! We've all been worried that you might decide not to come back and stay down south with your young man, but poor Charlie has taken it the hardest. I've not seen him so down in the dumps since…well…a few years now." Rose knew she had said too much and stopped talking, lest she let the cat out of the bag.

Frankie didn't know how to respond at first, unable to comment on Charlie or how he felt until she had seen him and talked things through. She decided to stay on safer territory. "I'm staying in Bayscar, Rose. I've left Robert for good."

"Well, thank heavens for that, young lady. That man was a dislikable rogue if ever I saw one! I'm delighted you're staying with us, dear. That's excellent news indeed." Rose beamed at Frankie, leaving her in no doubt that the sentiment was sincere.

"Thanks, Rose. I'm thrilled too," said Frankie, as someone walked over and sat at the freshly cleared table outside the tearoom. "I'm going to head off and find Charlie. I'll see you soon!"

Walking away, Frankie reflected on what Rose had said about Charlie. Was it so obvious to everyone that Charlie liked her? How could it have been obvious to everyone else but not to her? There was no easy answer to the question, and instead, Frankie focused on looking for Charlie's truck in the hotel car park, but there was no sign of it.

Frustrated by the realisation that he must have left the village and that she would have to wait for him to come back, she decided to go for a walk. Within minutes, she was on the coastal path and making a beeline for her favourite bench. There were people everywhere, and it was by no means as isolated and peaceful as it had been when she'd first found it in January. Still, as she sat down and closed her eyes, the gulls crying overhead and the gentle warm breeze on her cheeks soothed her and brought about the peace and tranquillity she was seeking.

Being unable to find Charlie was annoying, but in her newly calm and centred state, Frankie could see that having a few moments to reflect and gather her thoughts before she saw him was almost certainly a good idea. She had travelled such a huge emotional distance in less than two hours. Not to mention the distance she had travelled since she arrived at Robert's house for breakfast. In the course of one day, she had become excited at the prospect of motherhood, almost committed her life to Robert, walked away from Robert and accepted that life with Charlie and Lilly together was better than life without them. And now, she was facing the reality that Charlie was in love with her!

A teenage couple walked past, chattering and laughing, and Frankie watched them pass. Her mind drifted back to the pub car park, less than 24 hours earlier, and the idea of her teenage self being besotted with Charlie as a pop star pin-up. The thought made her smile, and slowly, the idea that she was besotted with Charlie, even as a rugged Yorkshire farmer, settled in and made itself comfortable at last. It was impossible for her to talk herself down anymore. This wasn't about Charlie being kind or helping her with the cottage, this wasn't about him being a distraction from Robert, and this wasn't about her needing someone to show her the love that Robert hadn't. Every word of context, every dismissal, every denial of how she felt about Charlie rushed from her mind and disappeared into the ether.

"I'm in love with Charlie," she said aloud, breaking into a wide grin for the benefit of no one but herself.

When she walked into the cottage in the late afternoon, all Frankie could hear was silence, and although there was still no sign of his truck outside, a small part of her was hopeful that Charlie might have walked up the hill to do some last-minute work on the decking and so be there to welcome her home. As she stepped into the lounge, knowing for the first time that this was her home, she smiled. Building a life here, in this house, perched high on a cliff, was a dream come true and so much more than she could have hoped for back in the dark days of January.

She walked through to the bedroom and noticed an empty coffee mug on the floor by the door, left by Charlie, and it made her smile. Opening the door, she walked out onto the deck. When Frankie had left the cottage on Wednesday, it had been rotten in places, in dire need of re-staining and the rail around the sides needed to be secured properly. But as Frankie stepped out, it was apparent to her that Lilly had been telling the truth because the entire thing had been replaced. It must have taken Charlie hours to construct, and it looked stunning.

He had left everything tidy, and no tools were lying around, meaning he had packed up and left. She had missed him. Sighing deeply, she leaned against the rail and ran her hand along, taking in the texture of the wood as she looked out across the fields and to the sea beyond. The contrast between the late afternoon sun setting over the North Sea and a playing field in suburbia was immense. There was no way she could have settled in Buckinghamshire again, having lived in Bayscar for five months. The village, the people and the scenery had seared themselves onto Frankie's heart. She was home.

After a while, the novelty of the decking paled in comparison to her thirst and hunger, and reluctantly, Frankie stepped back inside and got changed into a t-shirt and joggers before heading into the kitchen in search of sustenance. Once in the kitchen, she noticed that Charlie had used several mugs and washed them all, leaving them to drain and giving Frankie another clue about how many hours he had spent working on the decking while she was away. She ran her finger around the rim of her own mug as the kettle boiled and wondered where he was. There was so much she wanted to say to him.

A while later, Frankie curled up to watch TV, keeping an eye on her phone in case she heard from Lilly or, more importantly, Charlie. She was so engrossed in one of the property renovations shows she loved so much that she didn't hear the truck pull up outside the cottage, the key turn in the lock or the front door open in the kitchen. As the lounge door opened, Frankie jumped and spun around to see who it was.

"I wasn't expecting you to come home today?" said Charlie, standing in the doorway, placing his jacket on the arm of a settee. "I wasn't expecting you to come home at all," he added, alluding to his belief that she would stay with Robert.

"Well, this is my home. Where else would I be?" Frankie's heart pounded in her chest at the sight of him as she stood and walked over to the table to lay down her plate and mug.

Charlie moved into the living room, not taking his eyes

from Frankie's. As the sun dropped low in the window behind her, her hair glistened, and he could see the form of her waist through the thin t-shirt she was wearing. One of the things he loved most about Frankie was that she had no idea just how incredibly gorgeous she was. And there were a million things he loved about Frankie.

Frankie watched as he moved towards her, his arms tanned and muscular, his hair messy and oh so sexy, and those eyes. She wanted to drown in Charlie's eyes.

"You aren't wearing your wedding ring…." she said quietly, unable to think of a single better thing to say.

"I told you last weekend, at the hospital, that I was ready to take it off."

Frankie swallowed. "You did. I thought it was because you wanted Lilly." She felt ridiculous as soon as she said it, but it was too late to take it back.

Charlie just smiled. "It wasn't because I wanted Lilly. And while we're on the subject of wanting people, I thought you were going back to Robert?"

Frankie quickly explained what had happened just hours earlier, skipping the parts where she was thinking about Charlie, talking about Charlie, or driving home to be near Charlie. It didn't take long with all the 'Charlie' stripped out.

"You've had quite a day then?" he asked, still holding eye contact and sending Frankie weak at the knees.

"In more ways than one. I walked in on Lilly and Annabel earlier too!" At this, Frankie giggled, and the tension of the moment lessened a fraction.

"So, she's told you?"

"Yeah, she told me. And she told me you've been a true friend to her since she arrived, keeping her secret and supporting her…."

"Is that all she told you?" Charlie asked, stepping a little closer.

Frankie wasn't sure what to say. She didn't want to get Lilly into trouble, yet as Charlie stood within touching distance, all she wanted - no, needed - to do was be honest. There had been so much misunderstanding, so many assumptions, and incorrectly drawn conclusions. Whatever happened next (and Frankie had some excellent suggestions), it had to be based on honesty and trust. So much of her relationship with Robert was based on lies. Any life created here needed to be built on a foundation of honesty. There could be no other way for Frankie to thrive. And she so badly wanted to thrive.

"She also told me that you had feelings for me." It came out far too formally, and Frankie wasn't sure why. Nerves perhaps?

Charlie stepped away, and the delicate spell that was building between them was unexpectedly broken.

"Would you like to come and see the deck? I finished it earlier," he said simply, leaving Frankie astonished by the shift in subject.

"Okay," she replied, pretending she hadn't already checked it out and following as he led the way through the cottage and out into the early evening sunshine.

"I can't believe you did all this! In three days too!" Frankie exclaimed, genuinely impressed even on a second viewing.

"It was my pleasure to do it. I wanted to do something to keep me busy…."

"Surely the farm does that?" Frankie said, the nervous giggle making an unwelcome reappearance.

"Oh, it does, but I needed to be really busy. I needed to take my mind off the fact you were going down there to see Robert." As he spoke, Charlie watched Frankie, unable to take his eyes off her after so many hours of wanting her to come back, willing her to leave Robert and choose a life with him.

Frankie didn't know what to say and instead stood awkwardly, running her hand along the new railing. Charlie reached out and placed his hand upon hers.

"Is it really over between you and Robert?" he asked, so softly Frankie could barely hear him.

"It is," she replied simply.

Charlie cleared his throat. "In that case, there are some things I need to say to you. But I need to be absolutely sure that you are here to stay?"

"I am."

Frankie stood perfectly still, her hand still encased by Charlie's, and it was all she could do to keep herself from quivering from head to toe. He was so close, and the memory of his body held against hers swept in once more, pushing her dangerously close to losing her cool and simply throwing herself into his arms.

Charlie hesitated for a moment as if weighing up whether he could risk sharing the depth of his feelings. He gazed into Frankie's eyes as if searching for some kind of sign that it was safe to proceed.

"Charlie," Frankie began, aware of his hesitation. "I am here to stay. This is my home now. You are my home now. If you want…."

Emboldened by Frankie's words, Charlie cut her off, unable to hold back a moment longer. "When I first met you that day in the field, I couldn't believe someone like you had walked into my life…."

Frankie smiled, remembering how he had come across when they first met - disapproving and unimpressed. Little had she realised.

Charlie continued, "I couldn't believe someone as beautiful as you had arrived in the village. There was a sadness about you that I wanted so badly to take away. From the instant we met, I have had the strongest urge to wrap my arms around you and keep you safe."

Frankie closed her eyes, the irony of his words burning into her heart, her body now aching for him to do just that, and hold her.

"Every moment we've spent together has only bewitched me even more. I find myself able to talk to you and share things with you in ways I haven't felt comfortable doing.... since Katie. But it's scared me too, Frankie. I have never felt able to open my heart since I lost Katie. I've never even wanted to try. But when that man grabbed you in the bar, I wanted to rip his head off, right there. Holding you so close to me that night proved to me that everything I was trying to push away, everything I was trying to resist, was just pointless. I knew as I held you that I loved you, and there was no denying it anymore."

Frankie's mind was spinning, running through every moment they'd shared, looking for signs, and finding more connection and more emotion between them than she had ever noticed before. She had been doing precisely what Charlie was doing - pushing the idea of loving him away, fearful of what it might mean.

"And then I went back to Robert...." She said aloud, the culmination of her own appraisal matching his own.

"I didn't dare to tell you how I felt about you, and even in the hospital, when I held out my wedding ring, I still couldn't bring myself to be honest with you - or me! - about how I felt."

"And I was so positive about going back to Robert," Frankie added quietly, as the pieces fell into place for her. "Any hope you had of finding the courage was extinguished by my efforts to persuade myself that I wasn't falling in love with you. And then I left."

"But you came back," Charlie added, his eyes piecing Frankie's soul with their sincerity and love.

"I came back for you, Charlie. I can see it now. I was too scared to see it before. Too scared of what it might mean. For us both."

Charlie leaned down, and their lips met in the gentlest of kisses, and at last, he wrapped his arms around her and pulled her close.

As the sun finally set, the horizon ablaze with every shade of orange, all perfectly reflected in the stillness of the bay, Frankie raised her wine glass to the sky.

"Thank you, Grandma. I know this was exactly what you planned for me."

Charlie stepped out onto the deck. "Who are you talking to?"

"If I tell you, you have to promise not to laugh, okay?"

"I promise," he replied, placing a kiss on the end of Frankie's nose and making her smile.

"I'm talking to my grandma. Telling her about us." Frankie blushed, and Charlie put his arm around her waist.

"I think she knows about us, Frankie."

"What do you mean?"

"Put it this way, never before have I met someone I wanted to treasure like I want to treasure you. To hold you and shower you with the love you deserve to feel. From the first moment I saw you, I knew that the light in your eyes was the first thing I wanted to see every morning of every day for the rest of my life. My purpose from this day onward is to cherish you. If that isn't some kind of divine intervention, I don't know what is."

Frankie was speechless, the letter from her grandma echoing in her mind.

"I love you, Frankie Gleane. And I want to love you forever."

"I love you too, Charlie. So very much."

Epilogue

Frankie's eyes opened, and Charlie looked down at her, cradling their beautiful baby daughter.

"Frankie, meet Elizabeth." He knew she was exhausted after an arduous labour, but just at that moment, he thought she had never looked more beautiful.

Frankie smiled, tears rolling down her cheeks, coming to terms with the maelstrom of emotions flying around her mind. "Have you let Mum and Dad know?"

He nodded and confirmed they would come up to see her and their new grandchild the following day.

"There's someone else here who'd like to see you," Charlie's eyes moved to the door, and Frankie followed them until she saw Lilly, grinning like a proverbial Cheshire cat.

"How are you, sweetie? We missed you on Saturday. Our wedding simply wasn't the same without you there."

"I'm so sorry...." Frankie began, but Lilly wouldn't hear of it.

"Don't be soft! We'll have a celebration as soon as you're up to it. Never fear."

'I can't believe Annabel finally made an honest woman of you. I'm so happy for you both. I really am. Did your family all come along like you'd hoped?"

"They did, and it was amazing to have them all there, and

it all be so, well, normal! They all loved Annabel."

"I never doubted they would, Lilly. She is so lovely!"

"She is," replied Lilly, blushing. "Well, who'd have thought when we met two years ago that I'd be married and you'd be a mother by now? I still remember that awkward woman sitting waiting for her breakfast in the hotel, wondering what to do with her life. Look at you now, Frankie Gleane. All grown up!"

Frankie smiled, and they chatted for a little longer. But after a while, Lilly could see how tired Frankie looked and made her goodbyes, cooing over the baby in Charlie's arms as she did so.

"Happy?" Frankie asked as Lilly closed the door behind her.

"I'm not sure you need to ask. We have everything we could ever wish for and more. You are so beautiful, Frankie."

Frankie smiled up at Charlie as he placed the baby into her arms once more, allowing Frankie to take in the tiniest details of her daughter's beautiful face. Eyes shining with tears of joy, Frankie gazed at baby Elizabeth as she slept soundly, knowing with all her heart that the woman for whom her daughter was named would be smiling down upon them both.

Thank you so much for for reading 'Someone to Cherish You'.

I plan to release another book later this year, just in time for Christmas and I hope you'll consider following my Amazon Author page to receive updates in future.

Writing has always been a dream for me and in taking the time to read this book, you are helping me to realise that dream. I will always be grateful.

You can find more details about me and the books I am writing on my website.

www.ahbracken.com

Printed in Great Britain
by Amazon

79265761R00123